DESIRE IN FROST

CRYSTAL FROST BOOK TWO

ALICIA RADES

Published by PaperPlane Publishing.

Produced in the United States of America.

Cover design by Clarissa Yeo.

ISBN: 978-0-9914693-6-9

To Heather Wuske, who has been a cheerleader to my writing for years.

1

I knew the nightmare was coming before I closed my eyes. The same vision had been haunting my dreams for nearly a month, but as the weeks passed, I only witnessed it more frequently. By now, I was seeing Hope's abduction in my mind almost every night. I didn't want to face him again. I didn't want to feel Hope's terror as she was taken away. But I couldn't fight the fatigue any longer. I let my eyes droop, and then I drifted.

***

A hand clamped around my mouth, and my eyes shot open. My heart skipped a terrifying beat, and I began sweating under my covers. I wanted to open my mouth to scream, but the shadowed figure pressed down too hard against my face. Nothing came out.

An index finger hovered over the assailant's mouth, warning me that if I didn't stay quiet, there would be trouble. The room was eerily dark, but the moonlight outside my window illuminated a strip of his face. All I saw were green eyes staring back at me and the faint outline of his form cloaked in a black hoodie.

He picked me up gently from my bed, wrapping his arms around me, but he managed to keep one hand pressed against my mouth. It wasn't the comforting kind of hug my mother shared with me but the unfamiliar and terrifying kind I wanted to squirm away from. My six-year-old body was light, and I knew I couldn't fight my way out of this. I thought about screaming again so my mother would come to rescue me, but I was too petrified to make a sound. I didn't know what else to do. All I knew was that I couldn't fight him off. My body shook in fear, and a tear fell down my cheek. I prayed the stranger wouldn't hurt me.

The man cradled me in his arms and crawled back through my window the way he came. The pink lace curtains brushed against the top of my head as he pushed us both through the narrow space. He paused for a moment and released his grip on my mouth, but I was too frightened to make a peep. What was going to happen to me if I did? I didn't want to know the answer to that.

He quickly but quietly hurried across my yard toward the street, placing me in the front seat of a car I didn't recognize and shutting the door behind me. I caught a glimpse of myself in the side mirror. My young freckled face stared *back at me with big chocolate eyes.*

***

My blue eyes shot open. I breathed a sigh of relief, glad the nightmare was over again. My body was drenched in sweat, my heart was racing, and my covers were kicked to the foot of the bed. That's how it always was when I woke from this nightmare.

Like every morning this happened, I found myself wondering why. Why did I keep having the same dream about Hope without any new information to find her? This was one of the first dreams I'd had since I found out I was psychic a few weeks ago. If I had known what was happening then, I may have been able to save her. But the fact of the matter was that I didn't know what was happening then, and I was still confused, especially now that I was seeing something that happened weeks ago. My powers were supposed to help me find Hope, weren't they? So why weren't they giving me anything new to work with? All I saw was everything the police already knew.

I recalled the night of the Peyton Springs Halloween Festival when I visited my mom's fiancé, Teddy, at the police station. He knew my secret, so he asked if I could help find Hope. I remembered the way I felt and how my heart fell inside my chest when I looked at her picture. I recognized her.

"This girl went missing from her home recently,"

Teddy had told me. "Her name is Hope Ross. Of course, we're working with some larger departments on the case, but no one has made much leeway. The first 48 hours are crucial in an investigation like this, and we've already hit that time limit, but we still don't know much. We don't even know if she's still alive, but we're hopeful. I was wondering if maybe you could help us crack the case."

"I hope so," I remember telling him. "You'll have to give me some time, but I can tell you that I know she's still alive." I didn't know how I knew, but a flash of her face told me she was still breathing. Even weeks later, I still believed that wholeheartedly.

But I've spent too much time searching for her in my dreams! I cursed the universe. I kept seeing the same scene over and over with no new information that could lead me to her whereabouts. Since the police still hadn't found her, I was her only hope.

I curled into a ball on my bed and let a tear fall from my eye. I'd already helped people by using my newfound abilities, but I couldn't control them well yet. I could see minor things about people when I tried, but I could never see what I really wanted to see. With Hope, I didn't even know where to begin.

I'd tried different techniques, like looking into my crystal ball. Teddy even managed to snag one of Hope's beanie babies from her room—totally illegal, I know— so that I could touch something of Hope's and find her. So far, my gift of psychometry—finding things—was limited to lost books, CDs, and games of hide and seek. I didn't think I'd ever be able to find a person with this method.

Even when Teddy and I turned to Mom and her business partners, Sophie and Diane, who were also psychic, they hadn't seen anything. For some reason, my gift was stronger than all three of theirs put together. None of us knew why, but I had a theory. See, I'd only found out that I was psychic a few weeks ago, thanks to my mom hiding it from me for 15 years in hopes that I'd end up normal, but my abilities manifested on their own anyway. Looking back on it, I knew I had it in me all along. Maybe all the time I spent suppressing it and not knowing about it made it build up inside of me or something.

Without any concrete help from my mom and her friends, it was like everything that Hope was — and is — was frozen in time the night of her abduction.

A knock rapped at my bedroom door. "Crystal," my mom said gently. Without waiting for an answer, she opened my door a crack. "Are you awake?"

I quickly dashed the tear away before she could see me crying. I had told her I'd embraced my abilities. I didn't want her thinking I couldn't handle them.

"If you don't get up soon, you're going to be — sweetheart, what's wrong?"

I was never good at hiding my emotions, especially from my mother or my best friend Emma. I hated bothering my mom with my troubles. I mean, I knew she would help me and all, and she'd be more than supportive, but on some level, I felt like it was *my* responsibility.

I shrugged. Lying was out of the question. She knew me far too well, so I simply didn't say anything.

"Crystal, sweetie," my mom said. She crossed my room and sat at the end of my bed.

I rose to sit beside her. She took me in her arms and stroked my long dirty blonde hair. This only encouraged my emotions to run, and I sobbed into her arms. It felt like we had done this too many times since I'd discovered my powers, but I was glad she understood and could relate since she was psychic, too. The problem was that her abilities never seemed to give insight into the same situations as mine did, so she couldn't exactly help me on that end.

She didn't say anything; instead, she let me have my moment. When I was ready, I took a deep breath.

"It's Hope again, isn't it?" she asked.

I nodded. "I just can't figure it out." My voice cracked. "Like, what's the point of having this gift if it isn't leading me anywhere? I feel like I should have found her by now, but she just feels so far away."

"Crystal," my mother said with a tone of reassurance. "Our abilities aren't perfect. We're often shown what we need to see."

"But that's just it, Mom. I've seen the same thing night after night, and I'm not seeing anything new!"

My mother sighed. "Maybe you're just not looking

hard enough." She gave me a look as if to say, *That's a good point, you know.*

At first, I didn't believe her, but the more I thought about it, the more I realized she was right. I was always looking at the facts that were staring me in the face. I never took a chance to forget Hope's fears and really look at the peripheral of the scene. Maybe it was a good idea to open up to my mom more often so she could give me more insight like this. I thought about her suggestion—to look deeper—and wanted to try it, to see if I could pinpoint exactly what I was missing, but I didn't have a chance to investigate right now. I was going to be late for school if I didn't get my butt in gear.

I thanked my mother for her support and suggestion and then shooed her out of my room. I quickly got ready for school without bothering with makeup. I added my owl necklace—the one Teddy had given me when he proposed to my mom a couple of weeks ago—as a final touch.

At lunch that day, I found my seat next to Emma and Derek. I caught a glimpse of Kelli and Justine one table over and waved to them. After I used my psychic gift to rescue Kelli from an abusive relationship—with Justine's help—I'd grown close enough to them that I wasn't just an underclassman anymore. I was, on some level, a friend. Kelli smiled back at me. She seemed so happy now that Nate was gone. His mom didn't pull strings at the courthouse like we thought she would. She sent him to live with his dad instead so Kelli would be safe from him during his probation period, and hopefully long after. I could see it in her eyes that she was doing a lot better.

"You are so lucky," Emma raved.

I thought she was going to say something about how cool my abilities were again, something I had only told the people close to me. Sure, they seemed pretty awesome at times, but with the mystery of Hope Ross's abduction hanging over my head, I still had my uncertainties.

"How am I lucky?" I asked.

Derek looked at me like I'd just asked the dumbest question in the world. "You're kidding, right?" he asked. "You're leaving for Florida in the morning and get the whole week of Thanksgiving off. We only get two measly days off."

I must have lost track of the days because I hadn't realized it was already Friday. I hadn't even started packing yet. Sure, I was really looking forward to lazing on the sand at my future step-grandparents' beachside home, but I was afraid the trip would only complicate things with the responsibilities I felt toward Hope.

"Oh, yeah," I said flatly. I couldn't help it when a hint of uncertainty leaked into my tone. "Lucky."

2

"Emma," I complained. "I don't need this many outfits for just one week."

Emma was digging through my closet after school and tossing everything she thought I "needed" for my Thanksgiving vacation into a pile on my bed. Derek sat in my desk chair and laughed at us.

"Besides," I said, "we'll be in the car for most of the trip, so I should pack, like, athletic shorts or something comfortable, not all three of my swimsuits." I picked up my one piece and held it out to her as if that would explain my irritation.

"Oh, come on," Emma insisted. "You're going to be lying on the beach. You need a swimsuit so you can come back all tan. Why not this one?" Emma reached into my closet and held up the bright pink bikini she made me buy when we were shopping together last summer.

"A bikini? I've never even worn that thing. You're the one who made me buy it."

Emma rolled her eyes and tossed it back into my closet. "Yeah, so you could wear it for something like a trip to Florida."

"Why not this one?" I asked, holding up my tankini. "It's still a two-piece but a little more *appropriate*."

"Fine," Emma said. "Bring that one along, but I'm going to sneak your bikini in your bag anyway. You can leave your one-piece here." Emma shifted through some more clothes. "You might as well wear a sun dress while you're down there, too."

I sighed. "Okay. *One* sundress. I don't need four of them!" I didn't even know I had four sundresses. I reached for one of the dresses and placed it back on its hanger.

"Are you guys hungry?" Derek asked, running his fingers through his brown hair. "I'm hungry. Mind if I make us some sandwiches or something?"

My friends never had to ask to raid my kitchen. I nodded. "Sure. Sounds great."

Derek left the room.

I gazed at Emma as she watched him leave. Her eyes fixed on him, and her lips parted slightly and curled up at the ends, almost forming into a smile. When she turned back toward me, I was grinning in a teasing manner.

"What?" she asked defensively.

"Oh, don't think I didn't see that. You are so hot for him. I don't think I should ever leave you two alone," I laughed.

"Whatever," Emma said a little too high pitched. "I am not."

I kept my eyes fixed on her.

Emma crinkled her nose. Whenever she did that, it made her look like a chipmunk. "Is he cute? Okay, maybe a little. Is he, like, super nice? Yeah. But do I *like* him?" She paused. "But it's not me we should be talking about, Crystal. Are you okay?"

Emma caught me off guard.

I quickly dropped to my closet and pulled my duffel bag from the corner. "Yeah, I'm fine. Why?" My eyebrow began twitching. Emma knew that happened when I lied, so I always tried to turn away from her when I did. But I was a terrible liar. She could hear the dishonesty in my voice. I was sure of it.

"Crystal, we've known each other our whole lives. I can tell when something is bothering you." She paused for my response, but when I didn't say anything, she continued. "It's Hope again, isn't it?"

I finally turned to her and bit my lip. I'd confided with Emma about my dreams, but I never thought she'd be able to help me. Emma was thrilled about my abilities, and even though she wasn't born with the same gift, she'd been practicing "getting in touch with her inner psychic," as she called it. She came over almost every day for our "psychic exercises," her words, not mine, which consisted mostly of yoga and meditation.

As my mom explained, everyone is born with a sort of psychic ability, and all it took was practice—unless you were born with a stronger connection to the other side, like me.

Sometimes Emma would tell me more about things she read up on regarding the supernatural. I wasn't always sure what information to trust, so I'd spent some time with my mom at her Halloween-themed shop recently to learn more about being psychic. Even so, I didn't feel like I was getting anywhere new with my powers. Surprisingly, however, Emma had made quite a bit of progress in the last month. She was pretty accurate when she got feelings about a situation, which only made it harder for me to lie to her.

"Okay," I admitted. "Yeah, it's about Hope. It's just . . . I keep having this nightmare, and each time, I think it will continue and show me where she is or something, but it just stops when she gets in the car, and I don't know how to find her."

"Well, maybe if you tell me more about it, I can help," Emma offered.

"Come on, Emma. I can't tell you about the case." I wasn't actually supposed to know anything other than what was released by the media. I'm pretty sure Teddy had broken some laws by telling me what he knew, but he was convinced I could help him find Hope. At first, I thought I could, too, especially because I saw her in my dreams before she was even taken, but it had been weeks, and I still had nothing. In fact, no one had anything. Most everyone on the case had already given up.

Emma stared at me with her big brown eyes and played with a strand of curly dark hair. "Crystal, you know I've been getting better at this stuff. I just want to help."

She had a point. I mean, I knew she wouldn't tell anyone, and Teddy hadn't exactly made me promise anything.

"Okay," I caved.

We both took a seat on my bed, and I told her everything I knew. "Teddy says Hope's dad died right before she was abducted. It was a motorcycle accident." My voice caught in my throat for a second. I coughed to clear it.

Emma rested a hand on my shoulder. She understood far too well. My dad had died when I was around Hope's age, and to this day, the thought of death still got to me.

"Anyway," I continued, "the police have been on the guy's brother because of a mental history and a criminal background—I think it was just drugs and stuff like that—but Teddy doesn't think it's him. Well, they haven't actually found anything to tie the brother to Hope's abduction, but I'm thinking that maybe he was working with someone else or something."

"Why would he even take her?" Emma asked. "I mean, what's the point?"

"I asked the same thing. I guess the brother—Jeff, Teddy said his name was—has this thing against Hope's mom. When his brother Scott died, he thought he would be better for Hope than her mom was or something. I don't know . . . none of this really makes any sense to me. That was just the police's theory."

I paused to collect my breath. "Jeff does sound like a logical suspect, but Teddy said there was no ransom note and that after Scott's funeral, Jeff went back home somewhere south. They've checked all his credit card records and everything. But, I mean, it had to have been someone from the funeral, right? It was that same day, so it only makes sense."

Emma's lips pressed together in thought. "Why even treat it like a kidnapping, then? Couldn't she have run away?"

"Abduction," I corrected her. "I don't know, really. I imagine they looked into that possibility, but where would she go? If she was anywhere around town, they would have found her weeks ago. Her mom sent her to bed, and then she was just gone in the morning. Abduction makes sense. Plus, there's my vision that clearly shows she was abducted."

Emma rolled her eyes like that was obvious. "Yeah, well, the *police* don't know that. For all they know, she could have run away and slipped in the river."

"You're right, and I think some of them are giving

up because they're so clueless. I mean, Teddy won't say that to my face, but I get that feeling from him. It doesn't help that I'm not learning anything new about her, either."

"Didn't they dust for fingerprints or something?" Emma asked.

"I don't know. It's not like I was there with the police. If they did, they didn't find anything."

Just then, the doorbell rang. I had learned over the past few weeks to stay put whenever this happened. Emma would always stop me and say, "It's the perfect opportunity to practice your abilities!" She'd make me sit there and guess who it was, not that we had a lot of visitors. We did the same thing with phone calls and texts, too.

"I'll get it," Derek shouted from the kitchen.

Emma and I stayed put on my bed and both closed our eyes, trying to summon an image of the person at the door. When I saw his face in my mind, I groaned.

I still wasn't sure if Emma could actually do this or if she just guessed most of the time. "Who's the hunk?" Emma asked.

That's when I knew she was just guessing. "Hunk? Robin is *not* a hunk."

"Oh, it's *Robin*."

I wanted to slap the cheesy grin off her face.

"The hot musician who's going to be your step-cousin in a couple of months? You'll have plenty of time to 'get to know each other' on your trip." Emma wiggled her eyebrows suggestively.

I swatted at her lightly. "Shut up. For one, Robin is not hot. Two, he's hardly a musician. He just plays in a really dumb garage band. And three, ew! He's Teddy's nephew. Once Teddy marries my mom, that'd be, like, incest or something."

"Not really since you aren't blood related," Emma pointed out.

Robin lived in the city about an hour from Peyton Springs, but since he was coming with us to Florida, he came today so we could get on the road extra early the following morning.

I heard Derek and Robin shuffling down the hall. I rolled my eyes at Emma and took the opportunity to escape her teasing. I hopped up from the bed and exited my room.

Robin was taller than I remembered. He had short blonde hair that stood up in every direction and a little bit of stubble that, okay, I had to admit was a bit attractive. His blue eyes shone bright, and his features seemed to come together flawlessly.

But I didn't like him. He was always making some stupid joke at my expense. When Teddy first introduced us, I honestly had to ask, "Robin, as in Robin Hood?" because I didn't hear him right.

And then he spat back, "And you're Crystal, as in crystal meth?" And he was always picking on me for playing sports. Emma may have been right saying he was attractive, but the guy was a jerk.

"Um, you can stay in here," I told Robin, gesturing to the room next to mine. It was usually an office, but we added the fold up cot for him to sleep on that night.

He smiled at me, which was weird because, like I said, the guy was a jerk. "Hi, Crystal," he said.

"Um, yeah. Hi." I didn't know how else to greet him. "Did your parents drop you off?"

Robin's parents weren't coming because neither of them could get off work, but Teddy had invited Robin along anyway to come see his grandparents with us.

He pushed his way into the guest room and dropped his bag. Then he turned and jingled his keys at me. "I can drive, you know."

"Oh," is all I could say. Right. Robin was 17. I was briefly reminded that I was the only one in the house who still couldn't drive.

Robin slipped off his jacket. Underneath it, he was wearing a short sleeve shirt that gave me a nice glimpse of his muscles.

I looked him up and down for a moment and then realized what I was doing. "Uh . . . make yourself comfortable," I said with a half-hearted smile before fleeing the room.

3

The next morning, I woke with relief that I hadn't dreamt the previous night. Even so, it was a restless sleep, so I was tired. I slumped down the hallway with my duffel bag and purse and loaded them into the car.

I settled in my spot behind the driver's seat and fitted a pillow between my head and the door. Everyone else piled into the car quietly since it was early and we were still sleepy, but soon enough, we were on our way to Florida.

I didn't like the idea of facing Hope's abduction in my dreams, but I figured I was safe to rest my eyes. I must have drifted off because when my eyes flung open, I was in Hope's bed again, being silenced by her abductor's grip and then carried out through the window and placed in the car like normal.

Somewhere in the back of my conscious mind, I remembered what my mom had said. I had to look deeper, to forget the fright I was feeling and to seek further clues. The Crystal part of me struggled to break through the barrier that made me feel like Crystal on one side and Hope on the other. Was I Crystal, or was I Hope? While in the dream, I could never tell.

But then, for a brief moment, the Crystal part of me did break through. It didn't last long, and it wasn't enough to notice anything particular, but for a second, I knew who I really was.

My body gave a start, and I woke back in the car with my family. We had already made it from southern Minnesota to the flat terrain of Iowa. I slowed my breathing and stared out the window at the passing corn fields. It wasn't much to look at. Since it was the end of November, all the greenery I enjoyed about the area was replaced with a dull brown pallet. A light layer of snow dusted the corn fields. It was still early morning. I couldn't spot the sun, but I knew it was hiding somewhere behind the clouds.

It made me feel the way Hope was feeling right now. I didn't know how, but I could feel her sometimes. I knew when she was lonely and when she was hungry and when she was sad. Right now, Hope was feeling sorrowful, and the gray November sky seemed to mirror her emotions.

My stomach sank in response, and guilt consumed me. I still hadn't found her, and I was running away from the place where she had been taken when I knew she needed me. But what more could I do? I couldn't just put my life completely on hold and refuse the trip in hopes that I'd find something new in the next week that I hadn't seen in the past month. Besides, both Mom and Emma kept telling me I needed to relax. It's not that they weren't concerned about Hope. It's just that my gift worked better when I wasn't constantly worrying.

From next to me on the back seat, Robin pulled his earbuds from his ears. He looked at me with an expression I couldn't quite read. Disgust, maybe?

"Are you okay?" he asked.

I blinked a few times. Did Robin just show concern for me? Maybe he had matured a bit since I last met him. I almost cracked a smile at the thought that he might be a decent guy.

Normally I would tell people I was fine, but I found myself saying, "Just a nightmare that's been bothering me. Why?" I wasn't good at lying, but I had a way of bending the truth so I didn't feel so bad about misguiding people. Yet it surprised me that the full truth was coming out of my mouth, especially since I was speaking to Robin.

"Well, it's just, you kind of look like you're miserable, and it's bringing the whole mood in the car down. Let's try not to suffer through this trip, okay?"

My jaw almost dropped. Okay. There goes the idea that Robin might be nice for a change.

We rode in silence, and everyone attended to their

own devices or watched the scenery to kill time. I spent most of the day with my nose in a book. I wasn't usually one for reading, but it helped take my mind off things. I texted Emma and Derek a bit, but I had only been gone for a few hours, so there wasn't anything new to talk about. I glanced over at Robin a few times. Each time I did, he had his earbuds in and was texting someone. I wondered if maybe it was his girlfriend.

Looking at Robin, I found myself curious to know if he had some sort of ability like I did. I was thrilled that I had my mom by my side, and it was cool to know that Teddy was intuitive, something I had learned last Halloween. I loved the support Emma gave me, too. But what if Teddy's strong intuition came from somewhere in his family's lineage? What if Robin inherited that, too? It would be different with him. I'd have someone my age who understood the awkward stage I was going through.

Sure, I had Emma, but she wasn't born with an ability like I was. She was preparing herself and practicing her intuition whereas my gift was sprung on me from out of nowhere. Would Robin understand that feeling? I knew I couldn't just *ask* him straight out, so I turned back to my book.

In the late afternoon, Teddy decided it was time to stop for the night. I thought it was a little early for turning in, but I was glad to stretch my legs.

Teddy pulled off an exit and into the parking lot of a rundown motel. The paint on the side of the building was peeling, and the parking lot was riddled with cracks that weeds had started growing through. Each room had a door that led straight onto the sidewalk.

"*This* is where we're staying for the night?" I asked in disbelief. I mean, our budget wasn't *that* low for this vacation, and I knew Teddy's parents were helping us cover some of the costs.

My mother looked at me with a disapproving glare. "Crystal," was all she said, but it was enough of a reprimand to get me to shut up.

"I think it looks cozy," Robin said as he got out of the car and looked around.

Teddy opened his door and walked toward the front office to check in.

"Mom," I said once we were alone. "What is this? This looks like the kind of place where they don't wash the sheets and people get bed bugs and stuff."

My mom shifted in her seat to look at me. She was a gentle woman who was more like a friend to me than a mother. It seemed that since the engagement, however, she had been taking sides with Teddy more and more. It's not that I argued with either of them often, though. We actually all got along great.

My mom just looked at me and said, "Well, don't let them bite." Then she turned back toward the front of the car and laughed at her own joke.

I wanted to give her a look of disapproval behind her back, but her light mood made even me giggle at her dumb joke.

I scanned the streets. I still wasn't sure about the place. It just didn't sit well with me. Everything around here looked run down. There was a gas station across the street closer to the highway and a fast food place up the road. A small family diner sat next to the motel, but I didn't see many people around, as if this was a dying town despite its proximity to the highway. My gaze wandered farther down the landscape.

That's when my eyes fell on Teddy through the windows that led to the motel's office. I noticed motion as he slid something into his pocket. *That wasn't his wallet,* I thought. *It was — oh, my gosh. Did Teddy just flash his badge?*

"I'm going to — um — stretch my legs," I told my mom, which wasn't a complete lie.

I opened my door and began walking to no place in particular. I stole a glance at my mother, who was reading her book while she waited for Teddy. Robin was facing away from me studying the scenery, which wasn't much to see in this tiny little town.

I slunk around the building and stayed low so Teddy wouldn't see me. I pressed my body against the side of the motel and peeked in a window. My heart pounded in my chest. I'd never been very good at or confident in sneaking around. I was always too afraid I'd get caught, but I challenged the situation anyway and kept my eyes fixed on the scene before me.

I was close to Teddy now, so close that I saw him slide a photograph across the counter toward the attendant. The man picked it up, looked at it, and then handed it back to Teddy. I caught a glimpse of the image when Teddy took it back. It was a photograph of a man with short hair, cut almost to his scalp, and dark brows that a pair of menacing eyes looked up from under.

What is Teddy doing? I wondered. *He's not supposed to be investigating a case. He's supposed to be on vacation!*

The man behind the counter shook his head and then pointed to a high spot in the corner of the room. I followed Teddy's gaze and noticed a security camera attached to that spot on the ceiling. I was shocked a place like this even had a security system.

They exchanged a few more words I couldn't hear, and then I watched Teddy slide his credit card across the counter, thanking the attendant. He started to leave.

I circled around the building the opposite way I'd come so it wouldn't look like I was roaming around near the office. It was clear along the length of the building, so I took off running to get blood flowing to my legs. It felt fantastic after spending all day cooped up in the car. When I arrived back at our vehicle, I was huffing.

"Where did you run off to, Kiddo?" Teddy asked kindly.

I shrugged. "Just needed to stretch my legs."

Robin scowled at me, although I wasn't entirely sure why.

I didn't know how long I stayed awake that night in our motel room afraid to face Hope's abduction again. When I finally fell asleep next to my mother, I was extra tired as I felt Hope's and my own fatigue stronger than ever.

4

I woke to the familiar chime of my cell phone. I was sweating again and had relived Hope's abduction one more time, yet I hadn't seen anything new. I had tried, but I hadn't broken through that barrier that distinguished Hope from me. I knew I would get it with more practice, but that still meant waking up terrified each morning.

Sometime during the night, I had thrown the covers off me, so they were now doubled up in a heap on my mother's sleeping body. I fumbled around for my phone on the nightstand and prayed it hadn't woken anyone else. Robin stirred from the bed next to mine. I looked over at my mother on my own bed. She was still sound asleep.

I turned the volume on my phone to silent so I

wouldn't wake anyone and then checked the text I'd just received.

Rise and shine! It was from Emma.

What? I replied. I looked around the room. It was still dark. The only light seeped in through the curtains from a nearby street lamp.

It's yoga time. You promised we'd keep up while you were gone.

Oh. Right. I guess I hadn't realized she'd want to do it at the break of dawn. I sighed. She had really thought this through. I mean, we couldn't exactly share a yoga session while I was in the car the rest of the day.

I swung my feet over the edge of the rather uncomfortable bed and stretched my arms above my head, careful not to make too much noise. I tiptoed to my bag, pulled out my laptop, and unrolled my yoga mat—the one with an owl design on it that I had bought just weeks ago when we started these sessions—near the bathroom. The room we were staying in had a wall separating the sink area from the rest of the room, so I tried to get a little privacy behind it.

I fired up my computer and immediately received a video chat call from Emma. Her face glitched across the screen, an indication of the poor Internet connection.

"So?" Emma asked, her tone full of anticipation. About what, I didn't know.

"So, what?" I asked quietly.

"Duh." She rolled her eyes. "How's Robin? You can't go on a vacation with a guy like that without something interesting happening."

"Emma, he's practically my cousin," I whispered. "That would be so gross. Besides, I think he might have a girlfriend. He was texting her all day in the car yesterday."

Emma crinkled her nose in disappointment.

"So," I said, mirroring her tone in hopes that we could get off the subject of me and Robin. "What about you and Derek?"

"What?" Emma squeaked a little too loud.

I peeked my head around the corner to make sure she hadn't woken anyone. Everyone else was still asleep.

"There's nothing going on between me and Derek," she insisted, but I swore I could see her blushing, even if the video quality was poor. "Um . . . why don't we start our yoga session?"

I laughed a little inside at how she so quickly changed the subject.

Emma seemed to know what she was doing, so she was my guide for the day. I tried to make my legs bend in the right direction as she showed me new positions. The quiet, tranquil music she was playing through my speakers helped calm me, so I was relaxed when we finally said goodbye.

Emma had lectured me constantly the past few weeks about how important relaxation exercises could be when getting in touch with your "inner psychic." Although I was a bit reluctant to try them, I believed her.

Now that I was relaxed, I figured it would be easier to get in touch with Hope.

I thought about tiptoeing back across the room to get my crystal ball from my bag, but I didn't want to affect the "zone" I was in, so I just crossed my legs on my mat and set my mind on Hope. I felt like I sat there for quite some time, but after a while, I started to feel something. I never knew how I knew it, but I could feel exactly what Hope was feeling. I knew she missed her mom. This was the feeling I always got when I focused on Hope. But this time, something was different. The feeling was stronger. I wasn't sure if it was because Hope missed her mom more now than ever or if I was developing a stronger connection with her.

I sat there for another few minutes without feeling anything new except for a chill spreading out from my spine toward my fingertips. All my sweat had evaporated and left me cold. I longed to crawl under the covers next to my mother's warm body. I knew people would start waking up soon, so I ended my session by opening my eyes and pulling myself from the floor.

I glanced in the mirror as I stood and almost screamed. My heart jumped when I saw not only my face, which was fixed with terror, but a man with green eyes standing behind me. His expression wasn't one of malice, but he wasn't supposed to be there, and that made my pulse quicken at a threatening rate. I whirled around, ready to defend myself, but the man in the mirror was gone.

I gripped the edge of the sink countertop to steady myself as I slowed my breathing and frantically scanned the room. I nearly dropped to the floor when I realized I had just seen my third ghost.

5

After everyone woke, we piled in the car again and hit the road. It was just starting to get light out. I eyed Teddy from the backseat and wondered again what exactly he said to the desk attendant at our motel. Was the man in the photograph a suspect in one of his cases? Why would he have to ask someone so far away about a suspect in a case? Does Teddy even have *suspects*? Peyton Springs is pretty small, so I can't imagine he does much more than write parking tickets and respond to domestic disturbance calls.

I thought about taking a nap because I was bored, but I didn't want to face Hope's abduction again, especially when I was prone to thrashing around in my sleep while experiencing it. I didn't want Robin, who was sitting next to me in the back seat, to see that. It was embarrassing enough when my mother came into my room during the night to quiet me down.

The longer we drove, the more bored I became. My eyes fell on Robin, and I wondered if we could maybe do something together to ease my boredom, like actually have a decent conversation. But his earbuds were in, and he was texting again. I didn't want to bother him. I just opened my book and continued reading.

I was glad when we stopped at a gas station to stretch our legs. Mom and Teddy suggested each of us grab a snack to hold us over until we reached his parents'. I browsed the aisles and chose a package of trail mix and then met Mom and Teddy at the register.

"Did you use the bathroom?" my mom asked.

"Mom!" I glanced around.

"Well, I don't want to stop in an hour because you have to use the bathroom."

I sighed and handed her my bag of trail mix before heading to the bathroom.

A few minutes later, I stepped back into the main part of the gas station. I scanned the room, but my mom, Teddy, and Robin had already checked out. I caught a glimpse of them through the window. Robin was climbing into the car, and my mom was arranging herself in the front seat. Teddy was reaching in his pocket in search of the keys.

I began toward the exit doors to meet them at our vehicle. Then I saw something out of the corner of my eye that frightened me. My breath left my chest for a moment, and I had to do a double take down the aisle. There were two men standing there. One was a large man close to me browsing the chips. The other stood at the end of the aisle and stared back at me with green eyes.

I couldn't move for what felt like several long seconds. I only heard the pounding of my own heartbeat in my ears. My head spun, and I rested a hand against the store shelf to hold myself up. A shiver ran down my spine the same time my palms began sweating, throwing off the equilibrium in my body and making me feel faint.

The large man turned and crossed the aisle, blocking my view from the guy with green eyes, the one I was sure I'd seen earlier this morning in the mirror. *Green eyes just like the abductor*, I thought.

When my breath finally returned, I didn't wait another second. I wasn't quite sure what I was doing when I pushed past the large man in pursuit of the man in the mirror, but it didn't matter because he was gone.

The large man grunted and gave me a look that said, *What's wrong with you?*

"Sorry," I said, looking around the store again. And then I saw him. He had his back to me, but I watched him duck his head into a silver car.

I bolted. I wasn't thinking about what I was doing. All I knew was that if I was seeing this man, there were some questions—although I didn't know what they were yet—that needed answering. I prayed that those answers would lead me to Hope, wherever she was.

The man's car pulled out of the parking lot the same time I pushed my way out the door. I only stopped for a split second, and then I raced to my side of our car. My family met me with confused expressions.

"Him!" I shouted, pointing at the car that was getting away. "Teddy, follow him."

Everyone stared back at me blankly. Teddy and my mom exchanged a quick glance as if to say, *Do you know what she's talking about?*

"I saw him. Teddy, it's *him*." My eyes widened in urgency.

Suddenly, Teddy's expression shifted, and I knew he understood. He turned the key quickly and whipped out of the parking lot.

"Where'd he go?" Teddy practically shouted.

I didn't know. My heart pounded, and my breath quickened as I scanned the area for the gray car. We couldn't lose him! Then I spotted it. Desperation overcame me, clouding any other feelings, including rationality. "There!" I pointed.

Teddy stepped on the gas, whipping me back into my seat. He took the corner to the onramp a little too fast, and I slid into Robin. I caught my breath and looked up at him for a moment. His brow was furrowed, but he was surprisingly calm. I regained my composure—well, as much as I could muster—and slid across the seat and fumbled with my seat belt. Teddy weaved around a few cars until we were right on the guy's tail.

"Uh . . . Crap!" Teddy said under his breath.

I knew exactly how he felt. Now that we caught up with the guy, what were we going to do? I didn't have any time to think this through. All I knew was that this man was important and that I needed to get to him somehow.

Teddy whipped his body around to check his blind spot, and then he moved into the left lane. He stepped on the gas again until we were side by side with the gray car. Teddy honked his horn. He and my mom made frantic gestures from the front seat to get the guy to pull over.

I craned my head to look at him, but when I saw the man's confused expression and his brown eyes looking back at us, my heart sank to the deepest depths of my body.

Teddy honked the horn again.

I could hardly breathe. How could I have been so wrong about something like this? What was I thinking? Hadn't I said the guy I saw was a ghost? How could I think he could just get into a car and drive away?

"Teddy," I finally managed to choke out, only he was still honking the horn. "Teddy," I said a little louder.

He had his badge out and was holding it up to the window on my Mom's side of the car.

"Teddy!" I shouted as loud as I could. I wasn't one to shout, so I knew it surprised him.

The car went completely silent for a split second. "It's not him."

6

"What?"

My eyes brimmed with tears, and my throat closed up in embarrassment. "It's not him," I repeated, but my voice was so quiet that it felt like the words were sinking back into my chest.

Teddy dropped the hand that was holding his badge. He glanced at me in the mirror, and I could see his face tightening. Was he confused, or was he mad at me? I couldn't tell.

"What do you mean?"

I didn't like the sound of his voice. It was quick, deep, and critical.

Robin's and my mother's eyes bore into me. Teddy's were shifting between the road, the man in the car next to us, and me. I wanted to curl up in a ball that would swallow me and my disappointment whole. Maybe then I would be as small as I felt at that moment.

"I mean I made a mistake." My voice was just loud enough for them to hear, but I was too ashamed to raise it any louder. My throat closed up around my own words.

The car slowed as Teddy realized what I was saying. I caught a glimpse of his eyes in the rearview mirror. He looked mad. I mean, really mad. I'd never seen Teddy mad before, so I wasn't sure how to handle the situation. Teddy put on his blinker and merged into the right lane before taking the next exit. Nobody said a thing until Teddy stopped the car at another gas station.

My nose tingled as I fought back the tears I knew were coming. How could I have been so stupid? I tried to put the pieces together in my head. The abductor had green eyes. The man in the mirror had green eyes. The man in the gas station was the same man I saw in the mirror. I thought I saw him getting into a silver car, except I only saw the guy from the back. I was sure the man in the mirror was a ghost, what with him disappearing and the shiver I got both times I saw him. That means he couldn't have been the person I saw getting into the gray car. But he could be Hope's abductor . . . And that would mean—

"Crystal, *what* is going on?" Teddy demanded in a loud voice that pulled me from my thoughts.

A tear fell from my eye, and I quickly dashed it away. "I—I don't know." My voice cracked. "I saw him.

I was sure of it." I paused. All eyes were on me. Another tear rolled down my cheek. "I just—I'm sorry." I didn't know what else to say.

Teddy's mouth curled down in disappointment. He took a breath to calm himself. "Do you have any idea how embarrassing that was for me to flash my badge at someone who *wasn't* a suspect?"

Embarrassing for him? I was mortified for getting it all wrong. It was *my* fault. I couldn't tell if I was crying because I was mad at myself or because I feared Teddy's reaction. Either way, showing weakness like this in front of everyone in the car pulled at my self-esteem and made me only want to cry more.

"Next time, you better be 100 percent positive," Teddy warned.

A sob caught in my chest. I stared up at the ceiling in hopes that my tears subside, but I knew the tears were already written all over my face.

My mom touched Teddy's shoulder lightly to calm him down. He turned from me and exited the car. I watched him pace back and forth in the parking lot and then start walking toward the building.

I turned to face my mom and Robin. Robin's expression twisted into a cross of confusion and disappointment.

"What?" I snapped without intending to sound so bitter.

He looked at me for a few more seconds and then said, "I don't know what that was all about, but it sure sounds like you have issues." Then he unbuckled his seat belt and followed his uncle into the gas station.

I let the tears fall down my face. I didn't want to cry in front of Teddy and Robin, but right now, I wasn't shy about holding my tears back in front of my mom. She was the only one who would understand me. As much as I didn't want to show weakness, I knew she wouldn't chastise me for crying.

I couldn't quite explain what I was feeling. I was embarrassed for making Teddy chase after the wrong guy. I was furious that my abilities had failed me. I was frightened by the way Teddy reacted. And I was unsure if Teddy would ever trust me and my gift again. I knew Teddy didn't understand my mother's and my abilities — not to mention whatever mild intuition he had — but at least he trusted us. He trusted me enough to run after someone without a single explanation, and I had it wrong. What did that say about my powers and my judgment?

Most of all, little pins stung at my heart because I wasn't entirely sure how much I trusted my gift. That was what hurt the most.

My mother squeezed my hand to comfort me. "It's okay, sweetheart," she assured me.

I knew she understood on some level, but I had to wonder if her abilities had ever caused her to make such an utter fool out of herself. She'd told me that people had hurt her because of it and called her a witch, and that's why she never explained to me about psychics. If it skipped a generation with me, then I wouldn't have to face the ridicule, she'd said.

But did she ever feel this way about herself? Did she really know how a mistake like this bit at my self-esteem and ached my heart? I honestly didn't know the answer to that question.

"I just don't get it, Mom," I said. "I mean, I thought I saw the guy."

We both didn't speak for what seemed like forever. She just stared at me with a sympathetic expression in her eyes.

I took this time to again review the situation in my head. If the guy in the mirror was, in fact, Hope's abductor, that would mean that he was dead. That would mean that he couldn't have physically driven a car and that I mistook another man for him. But the fact that I saw the man with the green eyes in the first place means that he was trying to contact me about something. I knew that the farther south we traveled, the more I could feel Hope's emotions, yet I didn't know what that meant. I didn't know what any of it meant yet.

And then something small clicked in my mind. Finally, I broke the silence. "Mom, I'm starting to get the feeling that this trip isn't about Thanksgiving anymore." I met her gaze. "I think everything from here on out is going to be all about Hope."

7

Teddy and Robin returned. I could see Teddy stealing glances at me in the rearview mirror every so often as we drove. All I could see were his eyes, but I could still tell he was frowning. Each time I looked at Robin, he met my gaze with a scowl. At first, I almost thought he was mad at me, too, but it was so hard to tell with Robin.

Emma and I texted for a while, but I didn't tell her about what had happened. I felt reserved about the whole situation mostly because I was mad at myself about being misguided by my abilities. For the most part, texting Emma helped take my mind off it even though we didn't talk about anything important—and I liked it that way. It was an easy way to escape my worries. After a while, she had to go, and I was once again left alone with my thoughts.

Relief overcame me when we finally arrived at Teddy's parents' that evening. I could get out of the confined car and away from the scrutinizing glances — and perhaps clear my mind.

Teddy's parents' house was a quaint one-story home with the sand literally at their back door. A woman with salt and pepper hair and a big smile emerged from the house. She rushed toward us with her arms wide open as we all piled out of the car. Teddy embraced the woman and gave her a kiss on the cheek.

"Teddy," she smiled. "I'm so happy to see you!" She turned to me since I was closest to her. "You must be Crystal," she said. I expected her to shake my hand or something, but instead, she pulled me into a hug. "You can call me Gail. Oh, and Robin!" She circled around to the other side of the car to greet her grandson, leaving me a mere split second to react.

A half smile formed across my face. Gail's upbeat emotions and cheerful grin felt like a refreshing shift to my otherwise depressing day.

"Crystal," Teddy said, pulling me to full attention. His voice was soft again, but I could still hear a hint of something in it that told me he wasn't over what had happened earlier. I turned back toward him and found an older man standing next to him. "This is my dad, Wayne."

I forced a smile. "Hi."

And then he hugged me, too. Wayne and Gail

greeted my mother for the first time, and then they led us into their home for the grand tour, which wasn't much because it was only a two bedroom house. Mom and Teddy were going to stay in the guest room while Robin would sleep on the couch, Gail explained.

"Where do I stay?" I asked.

Gail led me to an enclosed porch at the rear of the house. "I hope this will do," she said kindly.

I looked around. The porch was small, but it was decorated tastefully with shell picture frames and a matching clock. The air was warm, and I could hear the waves crashing against the shore just out the window. There was an air mattress set up for me, which practically took up the whole porch, but I was happy to have my privacy.

"I love it," I told her in all honestly.

After we unpacked the car, Gail called us to the kitchen for dinner. I sat next to Robin and breathed in the sweet aroma of freshly baked dinner rolls.

Once we were all settled in our spots and we'd said grace, Teddy cleared his throat. "Mom, Dad," he addressed. All eyes turned to him in anticipation. I watched his face twist into a nervous expression just like the night he asked my mom to marry him. "I have some big news." He paused. He wrapped an arm around my mother and looked deep into her eyes.

Her gaze met his, and they locked onto each other. I loved seeing them together like that. It made me feel warm inside knowing that this was a part of my family.

Teddy's soft expression made it seem like he was less worried about what had happened earlier, and that helped calm me down, if only slightly.

The room went quiet for several long moments while Mom and Teddy exchanged a silent conversation—the kind I still wasn't completely able to decipher myself.

My mother finally broke their stare and shouted in excitement, "We're getting married!" Then she extended her left hand and showed her ring to Gail and Wayne. I noticed Robin sneak a glance at it, too.

Gail leapt from her chair and said something in such a high pitch that I couldn't quite understand her. She hugged both of them. Excitement emanated from the room as each face around the table filled in with a smile. I smiled at the announcement, too, even though I was there when Teddy proposed.

I twisted the owl pendant he had given me at the time around my fingers and thought back to that night. I liked how things could be so simple at times. Wayne and Gail asked a lot of questions of my mom, and she told them about her shop, Divination, only she left out the part about some of the things being useful to real psychics. We then talked about the wedding as we ate, and I let the happiness of the moment sink into my heart, hoping to keep this moment in my mind as I faced the inevitable trials of my psychic powers.

***

After we cleared our dishes, I finally found a moment alone with my mother. "Do you want to walk down to the beach with me?" I asked, hoping she would get the hint and accept my offer.

She smiled in reply.

My mother followed me down the stairs that led to the beach. I sat beside her in the sand and dug my exposed toes into it. Neither of us spoke for a long time. I grabbed a handful of sand and watched it fall through my fingers and back to the earth. Silence stretched between us as I mentally worked up the courage to confide in her.

"Mom," I finally spoke, but I didn't meet her gaze. "Have you ever used your abilities to help someone? I mean, to really help someone, like I did with Kelli and Olivia?"

"Oh, sweetheart," she said sympathetically, running a hand down through my blonde hair. "Is this about Hope? You're afraid you're not doing enough to help her, right?"

I knew my mother was intuitive, but she'd also told me that her psychic visions and feelings didn't work with her family members. That's how I knew she was speaking out of her motherly instinct, the one that taught her to understand me so well and to pick up on my emotions in a snap. I didn't always like when people could read my moods because it made it hard to lie, but at times like this, I was grateful my mother knew me well enough to understand me.

I lifted my head to look into her eyes. "That's just it, Mom. I haven't done *anything* to help her. I mean, I know I should use my gift to help people and everything, but it's just, sometimes I don't know what I'm doing."

"I know, sweetie." She ran a hand down my head again the way she always does when she's trying to comfort me. "Believe it or not, I do know how you feel. I've been called on to help people in the past, too."

I breathed a sigh of relief. At least I wasn't in this alone. "Really?" I asked, almost in admiration. My mom had been helping me over the past few weeks alongside Emma as I discovered more about my abilities, but only now did I realize that I didn't know that much about hers. I knew she could see pieces of the future and that she could find things through touch, but she hadn't told me much about her past as a psychic. Suddenly, I wanted to know.

"Who have you helped?" I asked.

"A few people," she answered vaguely.

Now I only felt like she was making me beg for information. "Like who? And how did you help them?" Maybe if I knew more about the people she'd helped, I could understand better how to help Hope and anyone else who came along.

"There was this guy once," she explained. "I had a dream—a vision—that he was going to die. For the longest time, I never knew what my dream meant. I didn't even know the guy at the time. In the end, my dream helped save his life."

I smiled at the thought that my mom was a real hero. Maybe I could be a real hero to Hope, too.

"Was it hard for you, you know, when you found out you were psychic?" I asked.

"That's where I have some regrets," she admitted. "You know my mom didn't have the gift but my grandma did. My grandma had always spoken to me about it, so when I started realizing that I had it, it wasn't completely confusing. My mom hated my grandma. I think she felt left out that my grandma and I were both psychic and she wasn't."

She sighed and then continued. "So I always thought it had skipped you like it skipped my mom. I didn't want to have an awful relationship with you like my mom and grandma did, and I wanted you to live a normal life. But now that I know you have the gift, I regret never telling you about it."

She'd mentioned this to me before, but she'd never delved into so much detail.

"I'm trying to be there for you as much as I can, sweetheart, but if there's one thing I remember when I was growing up, it's that I needed my space a lot of the time to think things through, so I'm trying to give that to you." Her hand came to grip mine in comfort. "But to answer your initial question, yes, it was hard for me, too."

I let this information sit in my mind for a minute, and then I moved onto a new question. "Have you ever saved someone who was abducted or kidnapped?" I asked, hoping her insight could help me here.

"Kidnapped? No, I haven't." She paused for a moment. "But with my experience, I've learned that psychic abilities can work in mysterious ways. You'll see what you need to see when you need to see it."

I thought about this for a second. "I don't know, Mom. Like you said before, maybe I'm just missing something. Maybe I'm supposed to be seeing something, but I'm just not. It gets really hard sometimes. Like tonight around the dinner table, everything was so happy and simple, and then the happy moment ended and my thoughts drifted back to Hope. And I feel I'm working myself up over something I have no control over, but at the same time, I feel guilty if I'm not worrying about her."

"Sweetie, I know you're scared, but the best advice I can give you is to stop worrying so much, face your abilities head-on, and wait for the answers to come. You can't control when or how you'll get answers, but you can control how you interpret them and use the information."

With that, my mother kissed me on the forehead and left me sitting on the beach alone. I could tell she left me so her last statement could sink in. So I let it.

8

Stop worrying so much. I repeated my mother's advice in my head while I walked back up the stairs to the house. I decided I needed something to take my mind off everything psychic related to actually make this possible. Just then, I spotted Robin exiting the back porch and coming my way. I figured a little criticism and snarky comments from him might do the trick. Or maybe there'd be enough human left in him that we could actually enjoy each other's company.

"Hey," I greeted.

To my surprise, Robin actually smiled at me in response.

"Where are you headed?" I asked.

"Actually," he said, running his hand through his hair, "I came out here looking for you. I don't really know what happened earlier today, but you seemed pretty upset about it. I just wanted to make sure you were still okay."

I almost fell back down the stairs I'd just walked up. Robin was concerned about me?

"I am okay," I assured him. "Want to . . . I don't know . . . walk down the beach or something?" I didn't understand why I couldn't formulate my words correctly or why I wouldn't meet his gaze.

"Sure," he said, once again taking me off guard.

"So," I started when we finally reached the sand. "I, uh, saw you texting a lot on our way down here. Is that, like, your girlfriend or something?" Why was I asking him this? I wasn't actually interested if he was single or not, was I? Or maybe I was just wondering because if I found out he was single, it would probably give him an excuse for being so bitter because, you know, he didn't have anyone to keep him company.

He laughed. "Or something."

Oh. So he did have a love interest.

"And you?" he asked. "You've been texting your boyfriend, too?"

I laughed so loud it was almost embarrassing. I quickly snapped my jaw tight. "Me? A boyfriend? No. That's just Emma and Derek. They're my best friends."

"Derek, huh?" Robin said in thought. "So you two aren't — "

"No!" I practically shouted. "I mean, I think he kind of has a thing for me, but I know Emma likes him. I could never date a guy my best friend likes." I tucked a strand of stray hair behind my ear.

We both went silent for a few moments until I spoke. "Don't you think the ocean is really pretty here?" The sun was already setting, but there was just enough light to enjoy the scenery.

He gazed out on the water. "Yeah, it is really pretty."

"I kind of want to stick my toes in it. Do you think it's cold?" I crossed ahead of him and approached the water. A small wave crashed at my feet. I squealed. "Yes, it's cold!"

Robin laughed from behind me.

"Aren't you going to stick your feet in?" I asked.

I glanced back at him only to notice that he was wearing long pants and still had his socks and shoes on. His sweatshirt hung unzipped around his shoulders. He shook his head. "No, I'm okay."

"You don't like the feeling of sand in your toes?" I asked, playfully digging my feet into the white powder that lined the beach.

Robin shrugged. "It's okay, I guess. Just not for me."

We walked along the beach until we couldn't quite see Wayne and Gail's house anymore. We eventually hit a pier next to a park, and lights from nearby houses illuminated our way until we made it to the end. We dangled our feet off the side and sat mostly in silence as we watched lights glitter off the water.

"This is nice," Robin said. Something about his tone seemed awkward, like he was forcing himself to be kind to me.

"Yeah," I agreed because I didn't know how else to respond. The hairs on my arms rose in response to the chilly air. I hadn't realized how cold it would get as soon as the sun set. I was still dressed in the shorts and t-shirt I wore on our way down here.

"You look cold," Robin pointed out.

I nodded. "I'll be fine, though."

"Are you sure? Because you can have my sweatshirt if you want it." He was already shrugging it off his shoulders before I could refuse.

I eyed him as he held it out to me, not daring to touch it.

"What?" he asked.

"Why are you being so nice? You've, like, never been nice to me."

He sighed. "I'm not being nice. Just put the sweatshirt on."

I didn't know where in his world he thought sharing his sweatshirt with me didn't constitute as "nice," but I couldn't reject his insistence. I took it and wrapped it around my shoulders, comforted slightly by its fresh smell.

We didn't talk about anything important while we sat there, and I was surprised that he hadn't asked more about what happened earlier. Eventually, we figured we should head back. At the house, we went our separate ways. It was only when I was crawling into bed that I realized Robin *had* taken my mind off Hope, if only briefly.

***

I opened my eyes to a room full of people. I wasn't sure how I got there. Practically everyone was dressed in black, and a few people were crying. I spun around to take in the scene. Chairs were lined up in rows on each side of the room, and I was standing along the center aisle. Almost every chair was taken. My eyes moved toward the front of the room, and that's when I saw a casket sitting there. It was closed and had a flower wreathe sitting on top of it.

For a moment, my breath caught in my chest as I thought about my father. And then I saw the picture of *him*, the man with green eyes who I saw in the mirror earlier that day. It was positioned near the casket and nearly took my breath away.

Oh. My. God, I thought, fixing my eyes on the photo. A strange vibe called to me from behind, willing me to look away. I turned slowly to investigate what exactly was tingling my senses. A woman with tears in her eyes sat in the back row. Her large red bun and black hat seemed to conceal the source of my feeling until she shifted and I spotted the man I was sure the strange vibe was coming from. His eyes were dark under his brows, and his hair was cropped short. My breath actually left my chest this time when I realized he was the same man in the picture Teddy had shown to the desk attendant at our motel.

His eyes shifted and focused on something toward the front of the room. I followed his gaze, and I had to swallow a lump in my throat before I could start breathing again. My eyes fell upon a little girl with short brown hair and big chocolate eyes who was fidgeting at the front of the room. For a moment, I was dumbfounded, completely paralyzed.

I regained as much composure as I could—which honestly wasn't much given the circumstances. "Hope!" I tried to say to get her attention, only nothing came out.

Suddenly, I understood what was going on. This was Hope's dad's funeral. The ghost I saw in the mirror and at the gas station was her dad, Scott, not Hope's abductor. And the man in the back was her uncle Jeff. I looked back at him again, studying his face. His eyes were still fixed on Hope.

"What did you do to her?" I wanted to shout, only there still wasn't any sound. No one reacted to my being there, but I already knew they wouldn't since I was looking into the past. But I didn't care. I was too overcome with anger and frustration. I clenched my hands into fists, and my body shook in rage. All I wanted to do was find Hope, and now I was staring into the eyes of her abductor. I was sure of it. That must have been what Scott came to warn me about—about his brother.

But I still needed answers. "Where is she?" I said, quietly at first to myself. Then, even though I knew no one would respond in a dream, I gritted my teeth and shouted the question at the top of my lungs.

A blood curdling scream tore me from my vision and jolted me awake. The scream continued, and only then did I realize it was my own.

My mom and Teddy rushed into the room.

I covered my face in embarrassment. I had never awoke from one of my nightmares screaming so loud and terrified like that before. Or was it anger? I couldn't fight it. A sob broke from my chest, and then suddenly, I was bawling into my hands. I curled my knees to my chest. My mother knelt beside my air mattress and wrapped her arms around me. Footsteps echoed outside the room just before Wayne and Gail hurried in to see what was wrong.

"Is she okay?" Gail asked.

"She'll be fine." I could still somehow hear Teddy's whispers over my sobs. "She just gets nightmares. It's fine. You can go back to bed. We'll handle it."

"Poor thing," Wayne said before he left.

Teddy closed the door to give the three of us privacy. I felt the mattress shift when he sat down and rubbed my shoulder for comfort. Even though I was crying, I was glad he was back to his sympathetic self.

My breath came in shallow heaves at first, but when I regained control of my body, I inhaled a deep breath to calm myself. "He took her," I finally said.

"Who, sweetie?" my mother asked. "Who took her?"

"Jeff," I said. "At the funeral, he was watching her. He was planning something. I just know it." I couldn't be wrong again. I just *couldn't*.

"Well," Teddy said, "he *was* our main suspect." I could hear it in his tone that he was forcing himself not to add, *But he's already been cleared*.

I took another few deep breaths to ease my cries. "I'm sorry to worry you guys."

"No, it's okay. We don't mind, Kiddo," Teddy assured me. "When you feel you have something you need to talk about, you know you can come to either of us, right?"

I met his gaze and nodded. I knew he was being honest with me, but I still wasn't sure how much he trusted my latest instinct. "Yeah, I know that. I just — there's no reason to worry you. The vision wasn't all that scary anyway. I think I was more angry than anything."

Mom and Teddy stayed to console me for quite some time, and then they said their goodnights and headed back toward their bedroom. I knew they were going to discuss the incident in private. Knowing they were just on the other side of the wall from me, I took advantage of this. I pressed my ear to the wall. Through muffled whispers, the only thing I could make out was Teddy saying, "My gut is still telling me it wasn't Jeff."

I wasn't sure if I was supposed to trust my own

intuition or his.

9

I was grateful when I woke and hadn't had another dream. Even so, I couldn't fight the knot in my chest that was full of concern for Hope. I had to find her. I just had to. I lay in bed for what must have been 20 minutes trying to sort through everything. I replayed the dream of the funeral in my mind, and suddenly, something occurred to me. I was aware it was a vision the whole time. Why could I see the peripheral details in that vision but not in the one of Hope's abduction?

I thought this through for several long minutes and realized that in Hope's abduction scenario, I was always in her head. At the funeral, I was a disembodied person looking down on the scene as if it were playing on a television. I knew I couldn't fall asleep and dream now because I wasn't tired, but I did know that when the opportunity presented itself, I had to look deeper into Hope's abduction and discover what I was missing.

After what felt like lying in bed forever, I decided there wasn't anything more I could do by staying under the covers. I threw on a pair of shorts and a t-shirt and listened to the ocean waves out the window. I checked my phone. Emma had already sent several texts reminding me about our morning stress relief session.

Sorry, I replied. *I just woke up.*

It was Monday morning, which meant Emma was already at school and I couldn't expect a text back for a few hours. I felt kind of bad for sleeping in through her texts. Emma was only trying to do me well.

I heard voices from the next room, but the ocean air called out to me. I decided to head down to the water instead of greeting my family immediately. I figured it would give me a chance to do some relaxation exercises like I'd promised Emma I would. Maybe it would even help me get in touch with Hope. I honestly didn't have a better option.

I sat along the bank with my legs crossed and my eyes closed. I tried to clear my mind, but thoughts of Hope, my friends back home, and even Robin kept creeping into my consciousness. I shifted to get more comfortable and then focused on the sound of the water and my own slowing breath while I let my mind drift in a realm that wasn't quite my own. It took several times of catching my mind wander before I finally let my body relax. I felt like I was floating, and my mind drifted on its own accord.

I miss my mommy, I thought. I didn't quite feel right. Nothing felt right, and I just wanted to go home.

"You hungry?" A voice whipped me out of my trance.

Hope, I thought. *She wants to go home.*

I looked up to find Robin standing above me. Even though it was morning, it was still hot out, much hotter than anything you'd feel in Minnesota at this time of year, so I was surprised to find him covered in long jeans. Didn't he get hot? It might be nice if he showed a little more skin every now and then.

Wait. What am I thinking?

"Huh?" I asked.

"Breakfast is ready." Instead of turning to head inside like I expected him to do, he lowered himself to sit next to me in the sand. "What were you doing?" His eyes locked on mine for a second.

I pushed a strand of dirty blonde hair behind my ear and stared at my feet in embarrassment. "I was, uh, meditating?" The statement came out sounding like a question.

"Mediating? You're not, like, a crazy wellness nut or something, are you?"

I should have known he'd have something rude to say, even if he didn't exactly hit it on the nose. "Uh, no. Not exactly. It just helps me relax."

"So, about what happened yesterday. I still don't really know why we were chasing that guy. I figure you know something about one of Teddy's cases that I don't, given that he was flashing his badge and all."

Whoa. I didn't realize he'd put the pieces together. I thought I had just come off looking insane.

"But," he continued, "whatever it was, I really respect you for following your intuition. Not a lot of people would do that."

My heart leapt in my chest. Did Robin just give me a compliment? That was a rare occurrence.

He ran his hands through the sand and looked down at the patterns he was making. "And I'm sorry for whatever I said to you about it before in the car. I don't even remember what I said. I do that a lot. I guess it's a defense mechanism or something."

My jaw dropped. I was speechless. Robin not only gave me a compliment, but he was also apologizing to me.

"Wow," I said with a hit of sarcasm and amazement. "Is Robin Simmons actually admitting that he's sorry for something he said? Who are you and what have you done with Robin?" I gave a little giggle.

But Robin didn't laugh back like I thought he would. Apparently we didn't share the same type of humor. Instead, he fixed his eyes on me and held an unamused expression on his face. "Stop being immature."

I immediately stopped laughing.

Okay, he was back to his old self. So much for thinking he might be a real human being.

He ran his fingers through his hair. "Did you not hear a thing I just said? Crystal, I'm insecure. I use my wit as a defense mechanism, but I don't take it well. It's hard enough sharing my feelings, especially around pretty girls, so just be glad that I apologized. Don't make fun of me for it."

Stunned, I didn't move for several long moments. I just stared after him while he retreated up the stairs slowly. My thoughts hung on the word "insecure." How could a guy like *that* be insecure? He was clever, and, okay, he was hot. What did he have to be insecure about? Only when he disappeared into the house did I rise from the sand and join my family for breakfast.

After breakfast, Mom, Gail, and I talked wedding plans, and Mom showed some ideas for the cake on her phone. I almost started thinking about Hope, but then I remembered that things were easier for everyone and I had a better chance of finding her when she was not at the forefront of my mind. I again basked in the simplicity of the wedding planning and offered my opinions when necessary.

Later, Wayne suggested we all go down to the tennis courts nearby and play a game. I thought this was a great idea until I realized that if everyone else was gone, I would have time to try connecting with Hope. I knew I had said it was best to keep my mind off her, but I really wanted some privacy with my crystal ball since I hadn't had a chance to use it yet after everything that happened. I kindly said I didn't want to go and excused myself to my guest room.

Once I heard the front door shut and a car pull out of the driveway, I pulled my crystal ball from my bag and set it on the floor in front of me. I took several long deep breaths to calm myself, and I held the owl pendant around my neck close to my heart for good luck. I stared deep into the ball. I had been able to make it work in the past, but I still struggled with it. I had an especially hard time clearing my mind.

No expectations, I reminded myself.

I used the sounds of the waves coming in my window as an anchor so I'd have something to focus on besides my racing thoughts. The minutes ticked by, and after a long time, colors began swirling in the ball. They became the center of my focus as I fell deeper into the unknown. A faint figure formed in the crystal ball. I almost thought I saw Hope's face, but then the image washed away as a chill settled over the room.

"Help!" A voice startled me. My eyes jerked up to find a young girl standing in the room.

My head began spinning. I was glad I was sitting down so I didn't have to find an extra support to keep myself upright. I was starting to understand this feeling all too well.

The girl had long dark hair and big beautiful eyes. For a second, I almost thought she was Hope. My heart sank at the thought that I'd failed her, but the girl standing in front of me was a lot older than Hope, just a few years younger than me.

I wanted to smile at her, to let her know that I wasn't a threat, that I could help her even. I didn't when I saw that the ghostly girl had an expression of urgency fixed to her face. My expression transformed to mirror hers when I realized that someone was likely in danger. I couldn't think of any other excuse for why this ghostly girl would show herself to me.

"You have to help her," she said. "She's been scared for so long. I just want to see her happy."

Now I knew for sure someone was in danger. *Calm down*, I told myself, but that was always difficult when a ghost was asking for help.

"Who?" I asked, a little bit louder than I intended. "Who do you need me to help?"

The girl looked around the room as if trying to take in her surroundings, and then her eyes fell back on me.

"My sister."

10

A knock at my door startled me.

"Crystal, are you okay?" asked a deep voice.

Robin.

My eyes jerked toward the door in surprise then back at the girl, but she was already gone. The chill that filled my body each time I saw a ghost subsided. I quickly shoved my crystal ball back into my bag and covered it up with a shirt just as Robin opened the door a crack.

"Can I come in?" he asked without looking.

I plopped onto my mattress to make it look like I was just relaxing. If he could hear my racing heartbeat—and I was almost paranoid that he could—it would undoubtedly give me away. "Yeah," I answered in a fairly normal tone. "I'm fine. I thought you went with everyone to play tennis." I picked at my fingernails so I wouldn't have to meet his gaze. I'd never been a good liar. At the same time, it would be far too difficult to explain to him what I had just been doing. No way would he believe I'd just encountered a ghost.

He scoffed, pushing his way farther onto the porch. "I've told you before, I don't play sports."

I looked him up and down. "Really? Because you're really — "

Wait. What was I just about to say?

Robin took a seat next to me on the air mattress. My heart sped up, and I realized how uncomfortable I was being so close to a guy. I'd never really had a boyfriend before, and I only ever hung out with Derek when Emma was around, so being alone with a male of any sort was out of the ordinary for me.

Robin smiled and raised his eyebrows. "I'm really what?"

I wanted to lie to him, but I couldn't come up with an alternative excuse. His stare encouraged me to explain. I spoke slowly, but my voice wavered. At least he would attribute that to my embarrassment instead of my anxiety over the ghost girl. "Uh . . . I was going to say muscular, but now that doesn't feel very appropriate." I added a slight teasing tone to my words, but I could still feel a blush rise to the surface of my cheeks when I spoke. It surprised me that I was able to admit something like this to him.

"Oh, you think I'm muscular?" he said, flexing his

bicep and looking down at it.

The gesture was in humor, but it only made me think, *Um, yes!*

"So," I said, hoping to change the subject. "If you don't play sports, what *do* you do?"

"I do weight lift a little, but nothing where I have to run around a court. Mostly, though, I play music."

"Oh, so you're in band? I play the clarinet."

Robin gave a sort of laugh that made me feel insecure about my choice of instrument. "I'm not in *the* band, Crystal. I am in *a* band."

"I knew that, but you're, like, not in band in school?"

He shook his head.

"So, are you in any extracurricular activities?"

"For me, it's just basically school and my band."

"And your girlfriend, right?" I said, only I regretted it immediately. Why did I have to say such stupid things sometimes? I ran my fingers through my hair and twisted it at the ends.

Robin simply laughed, but he didn't say anything about his girlfriend.

"So, what? You're just going to play music the rest of your life and hope you make it big?" I asked in an attempt to break the awkward silence stretching between us.

"Well, it's holding me over for now. We've had a few well-paying gigs. It's not much since we've bought some new equipment and I have to split the profit between four other guys, but it's helping me save up for college. I want to go into occupational therapy and help people who have been in accidents and stuff."

"Oh," is all I said, even though I wanted to tell him how noble that sounded.

"And you?"

It took me a few moments to realize what he was talking about. I was only 15 for goodness sakes. I hadn't really thought about what I wanted to do with my life. Maybe I could turn my psychic skills into some sort of practice, but I wasn't sure how I would make a living that way. I couldn't *charge* people to have me help them.

I played with the ends of my hair and said, "I want to help people. Kind of like a counselor or something." I shrugged like it wasn't a big deal, but I knew it kind of was. I hadn't thought about how my abilities were going to affect the rest of my life. I was still trying to make it through my sophomore year alive. "Anything else I should know about you?" I asked, wondering if he was going to show more of his human side.

He didn't. He just said nope and exited the room, leaving me to stare after him. I had a feeling he was hiding something from me. I wondered again if he inherited some of the intuition Teddy had and if that was what he was hiding from me.

Only when he was out of the room did I have a chance to think back to the girl who had come to me. Suddenly, it felt like all my responsibilities related to my gift were piling up again. I had to somehow find Hope, and God only knew I wasn't making any progress on that end. I probably had to talk with Scott's ghost again. After all, he had to be trying to contact me for a reason. And now I had a new ghost who wanted me to help someone else who I knew absolutely nothing about.

I fell back down on the air mattress and closed my eyes in an attempt to relieve my anxiety. I didn't fall asleep. Instead, I figured I should stop worrying about everything like my mom had suggested.

I spent most of the rest of the day lying on the beach in the sundress Emma insisted I bring along while enjoying the weather and reading a book. Diving into a different world was the best way I could think of to take my mind off everything. I had already finished the first two books in the series in the car, and I was onto the third. It was about a psychic girl, much like myself, named Sabine. We could do different things with our abilities, but I had a lot to learn from her character. At the same time, I found it easier to focus on her problems instead of my own since I wasn't getting anywhere by worrying.

At one point, I looked up toward the house to see if my mom and everyone else was home yet. I could have sworn I saw Robin looking out the window. I wasn't sure if he was watching me or if he was just enjoying the scenery.

After I finished my book, I walked back up to the house. Robin was still the only one home. It felt awkward with only us two in the house, like I was obligated to do something with him. When I entered the kitchen, he was sitting at the table shuffling through a deck of cards. A part of me wanted to talk to him, but another part of me felt like he didn't want me around. I was about to turn back toward the porch when he spoke.

"Want to play something?"

I almost looked around the room to make sure he was talking to me, but I already knew I was the only one there. I blinked a few times, shocked by his offer, before I found my voice. "I'm not very good at cards."

"Do you know how to play rummy?" He finally tore his gaze from the deck and looked up at me.

"Yeah," I said, slowly inching for the chair across from him.

"Play you to 500 points?"

I shrugged. "Why not?"

"We need something to keep score with," he pointed out.

I felt like a fool rummaging around the kitchen looking for a notepad and a pencil, but I eventually found both and took a seat across from him, sliding the pad and pencil his way. At the top, I watched him write Crystal Frost on one side and Robin on the other. Then he separated the sides into two columns.

"Why'd you write out my full name and only your first name?" I asked, pointing to the paper.

He shrugged. "I think your full name is really cool. It's like your first name is an adjective and your last name is a noun."

I had never thought of it that way before.

"I might just call you by your full name from now on," he said.

"Please don't," I begged. When I noticed he was smiling, I realized he was kidding. He stared across the table at me, and my cheeks flamed in response. Was he *flirting* with me? No. Not Robin. He wouldn't.

"Just deal the cards," I insisted.

We played for a long time, although it wasn't as great of a game with just two people, until eventually Robin won. Only after the game ended did I realize that I was smiling and laughing with him. I could hardly believe it.

Robin gathered the cards into a pile and started shuffling. "Rematch?"

"But you already won. Why would you need a rematch?"

His eyes bore into mine. "Maybe I don't want the game to end." Something about it sounded like a challenge, so I accepted.

Robin handed me the note pad and told me to keep score this time. I started by ripping the top sheet off and crumpling it into a ball. I scrawled my name first on a clean sheet, making a point to write just my first name, and then I added Robin's alongside mine. I could see him peeking at my writing from out of the corner of my eye.

"What is that?" he asked.

"Huh?" I looked up to meet his gaze.

"My name has an 'i' in it."

I glanced back down at my handwriting. I knew my handwriting had always been poor, and now Robin knew it, too. That meant he had something to make fun of me for. But I wouldn't let him use it against me.

I scowled at him. "I did put an 'i' in it!" I dug the pencil into the paper to accent the dot over the 'i.' "Yes, I have chicken scratch handwriting. Now, can we start the game?"

Robin called rummy on a card I placed in the discard pile on accident, but then I caught him doing the same thing later. We both grabbed a can of pop from the fridge and sipped on them and laughed at ourselves as the game continued. When I had a moment to really evaluate the situation, I was shocked at how much I was enjoying myself. I knew there was nothing particularly fantastic about the game, but something about playing with Robin made me loosen up a bit.

Robin won a second round just as everyone else arrived home. They were carrying in shopping bags, and I noticed Teddy had a box of leftover food from a restaurant. Clearly they'd spent the day doing more than playing tennis. A part of me didn't care that I wasn't included when I looked across the table at Robin and realized I'd actually had fun with him.

That night, I called Emma via video chat. I was a little surprised to see Derek in her room with her. Of course, her door was open and her little sister Kate was in there with them. I could see Kate in the background coloring on something on the floor. Still, it was either always just Emma and me or all three of us together. It made me feel kind of left out.

"How are you liking Florida?" Emma asked.

"The weather here is so nice," I raved.

"And the boys, too?" Emma asked.

"Emma!" I scolded at the same time Derek did. We all giggled.

"Crystal," Derek said. "You'll never believe what happened."

"Yeah," Emma agreed. "It's really pretty sad."

"What?" I asked, alarmed.

Emma looked at Derek. "You tell her."

Derek's eyes drooped in sadness. "My dog, Milo, ran away."

"Oh, no, Derek. That is really sad. I wish I could help."

"No, it's okay," he told me. "We've got it covered. Kate is drawing fliers for us to put around town so we can find out if anyone has seen him. The thing is, he slipped out of his collar, which is how he got away, so anyone who finds him won't know he belongs to us." I thought I could hear a sob cut at his tone.

I felt bad for Derek, and I told him so. He eventually turned away and crouched next to Kate on the floor to help her with the fliers.

"Is he going to be okay?" I asked Emma.

She looked back at him. "Yeah, I'm sure he will be.

If you were here, maybe you could work some of your magic."

I laughed a little because of the way she said it, but she was probably right. I had become quite good at finding things, but I had to have something to touch, like the dog's collar, to tell where he was.

"I'll work on it, but I probably won't find anything," I told her.

"Well, I've been trying my best, too," Emma said, "but I've never had experience with finding things. The best thing I can come up with is that I have a good feeling about a penny. Like, a lucky penny or something." She shrugged. "Except I don't think that it's about Derek's dog. I think it has to do with you."

11

That night, I dreamt about Hope. I was again in her body, being carried out her window by a man I still couldn't get full features of. I knew I had to become aware of my surroundings. I had to somehow find what I was missing, but when the Crystal part of me broke through, all I could do was scream in my own mind at the assailant.

"Where is she?" I cried, only I was watching a scene that happened weeks ago, and the man couldn't hear me.

I woke once again with a start. I was getting too used to this. I pulled my covers up from the foot of the bed and wrapped them around my body for comfort. I stayed in bed, closed my eyes, and controlled my breathing to calm myself.

"Oh, Hope," I whispered. "I wish I could help you. Where are you?" A tear fell down my cheek. "Why am I seeing you if I can't help you?" I wanted to shout it, but I didn't want anyone else to hear, so I kept my voice low.

A sob broke within me. I didn't fight it. All I wanted was to use my gift to help people, and I couldn't control it well enough to do so. My head ached. I pressed my face into my pillow and screamed.

"I just wish I could help you," I said again, squeezing my eyes shut to get all the tears out.

"Crystal," a voice called out.

My eyes shot open in surprise the same moment I bolted up in bed. My gaze fell upon the ghostly girl standing next to my air mattress. It was the same girl who had visited me yesterday. I wiped my eyes as my racing heart slowed. I couldn't refuse helping the girl, and I knew it, even if that did take me further from Hope.

I composed myself in a quick moment. "Can I help you?" I asked quietly but in a friendly tone.

She looked back at me with urgency. Her eyes weren't quite the same color as Hope's, but something in them reminded me of her.

"I just want to see my sister happy," she said.

I was getting fed up with the way ghosts spoke to me. They never seemed to give me a clear cut answer to the information I needed. But I stayed calm. "How can I help her? What's wrong with her?"

"I don't think she's safe. My mom has kind of . . .

gone crazy. She's not herself."

Oh no, I thought. I didn't like the sound of someone being in danger. It broke my heart. "Who are you?" After I asked it, I knew it wasn't the best question to ask since the girl probably didn't have much time here.

"I'm Penny."

"You're—" My breath caught.

I have a good feeling about a penny, Emma had said.

Not *a* penny. Just Penny.

"Penny?" I whispered.

If Emma was giving me clues about this girl before even *I* knew her name, there was something really important about her. I mean, I knew she was important because she'd shown herself to me, but something about the whole situation made her seem significant in a different way that I initially thought.

"You have to find hope," she said.

I almost broke out crying again. "Hope? I haven't had much of that lately."

"No," Penny said. "Not 'hope' as in faith. I mean Hope. My sister."

Suddenly, my vision blurred. Instead of sitting on Wayne and Gail's porch, I found myself in front of a small blue home. As soon as I saw it, the vision was gone. I was back on the porch again, but Penny was nowhere in sight.

***

My head spun. Penny had shown me where Hope was, and then she disappeared. I still couldn't believe that all this time I *was* getting closer to Hope. She was only about four hours north of here, and even though I didn't have an address, something inside of me knew exactly where to go.

When I could finally move again, I made my way to the kitchen. I found my mom and Teddy sitting at the table and Gail standing over the stove.

"Mom," I said quickly.

She and Teddy both looked up at me in alarm. "What's wrong, sweetheart?" she asked. "Are you okay?"

"No, not really," I admitted, taking a seat across from her. I kept my voice low, hoping Gail wasn't paying too much attention. "I know where Hope is. It's only about four hours away. We have to go find her."

Mom and Teddy both stared at me, but I couldn't quite read their expressions. I thought my mom's was one of sympathy and Teddy's was one of disbelief, but I wasn't entirely sure. Silence loomed over us for several long seconds as they stared back at me. It was like they hadn't even heard what I'd said.

"What are we waiting for? I finally have something!"

I wanted them to leap up in excitement and follow me to the place Penny had shown me. Instead, all they did was exchange a glance.

"Kiddo," Teddy said, setting down his newspaper

and folding his hands on top of it. He looked at me with all seriousness. "Are you sure about this?"

I nodded eagerly. "I'm positive."

Teddy twisted his face into an expression that could only be described as skepticism. "You can't just go chasing after a kidnapper."

I gaped at him. "But I have to."

Teddy shook his head lightly. "You don't. We can have someone else check it out. Someone who is trained and armed."

I furrowed my brow. "I—I don't know how to tell them where to go."

"What do you mean?" Teddy asked with a hint of annoyance in his voice. "You just said you knew where she was."

"I do. I can't explain it, though. It's like I'm drawn to the place, but I won't know how to get there until I'm there."

"Well, you said it's four hours away, so you know the general area. We can have someone in the county look into possible leads."

"And that could take days!" I exclaimed.

Teddy pursed his lips and went silent for several moments. When he finally lifted his gaze to meet mine, he spoke. "I don't think now is the time."

"What?" I practically shouted.

Gail turned to me from the stove, but I could tell by her expression that she didn't want to be a part of this argument. She tended to her food again to give us a minor amount of privacy.

"Teddy, I'm telling you I've found Hope, the girl you've been searching for for weeks, and all you can say is, 'It's not the time?'" My chest tightened when it hit me that I was right about Teddy. He wasn't going to trust me again.

"The thing is, Crystal, you were wrong last time, and I don't want to be sent on a wild goose chase. And we still don't have anything on Jeff. I think we should just enjoy our time here. We're on vacation. Enjoy yourself. Stop worrying."

There it was again. Everyone, it seemed, was telling me to stop worrying, but I didn't have the heart to do that without guilt pulling me down. Everything he'd just said made it feel like he'd reached into my chest and ripped my heart out. I could hardly breathe. My nose tingled at the threat of tears.

"What are you saying?" My voice cracked in response to my crushed heart. "That you don't believe me?"

He sighed. I'd never thought Teddy would treat me like this. He'd told me things about the case because he thought I could help him. Was he giving up on me? If he didn't believe me, how was I supposed to believe in myself?

"Crystal," he said through gritted teeth. "I'm just saying that I can't go barging into someone's house without probably cause. Right now, I have no evidence."

Something—I'm not sure if it was my psychic powers or if it was something in his eyes—told me that wasn't the real reason he didn't want to listen to me. The truth was that Teddy didn't trust me anymore.

I stood in rage. "You're the one who came down here looking for her! I saw you asking questions about Jeff at our motel. So why won't you follow me to Hope now?"

Teddy's voice rose slightly to mirror my own. "Crystal, I haven't given up on Hope. What you saw— I'm still trying to find her even though pretty much everyone else believes she's dead. The reason we stopped there was because we have credit card records showing that's where Jeff stayed after he left the funeral. *That* kind of evidence I can manage, but you're asking me to spend all day following a lead that makes no sense in the realm of science!"

This time, his words cut even deeper, which I didn't think was possible. Tension formed in my head, and it felt like a boa constrictor was wrapping its body around my skull and trying to crush it. I clutched at my stomach because in that moment, it felt completely empty. I thought Teddy believed in me. How could he say that about my gift?

My breath returned to my body. "She had an older sister! Did you know that?" I was shouting now. It was the only thing I could do after the way he was making me feel, like the biggest part of me didn't matter to him at all, like I was stupid and untrustworthy, like he didn't want to listen to anything I had to say.

"What? Hope? See, Crystal, that's why I can't go chasing after her. You were wrong about the man earlier, and you're wrong about Hope now. She was an only child."

I was momentarily struck dumb by this information. I knew I couldn't be wrong about this again, yet something in the back of my mind left me worried that I was. I managed to find my voice again. "She's dead, Teddy. Penny is dead, and she told me where to find Hope." I didn't even care at this point that Gail was hearing all about my abilities. All I knew was that I had to find Hope.

"I assure you that Hope was Melinda and Scott's only child."

I took a step back. I couldn't believe he was treating me like this. He didn't believe a word I'd said.

It brought worries to the forefront of my mind and made me wonder myself. *Their only child? That can't be right. Was Penny having me run after a different girl named Hope?* I blinked a few times as I processed this information.

My tone finally returned to its normal volume, but I spoke through gritted teeth. "Either way, there's a girl named Hope four hours from here who needs rescuing."

Teddy stared at me with an apologetic expression on his face, and then he spoke quietly. "Crystal, I'm sorry."

I knew that was the end of our conversation, although I wasn't entirely convinced that he *was* sorry. I stormed back through the enclosed porch and down the steps toward the beach. I took a seat in the sand and curled my knees to my chest while I sobbed into my arms. I tucked my head in close to my body, trying my best to make myself as small as I could to reflect the way I was feeling.

How could Teddy not believe me? He was the one who had asked for my help. I had assumed he believed in me. He'd said he had some heightened intuition of his own, so why was he pushing everything we both believed in away? Or was that the problem? Had my mistake made him so afraid of his own intuition that he no longer wanted to accept it as truth?

Several long minutes later, a hand touched my shoulder. I jerked up in surprise, ready to retaliate. I let my body relax when I saw that it was only my mother. She sat by me on the sand and pulled me into an embrace. I sobbed in her arms. I tried not to since it seemed like I'd been doing so much of that lately, but I couldn't help it. Someone was out there who needed my help, and I was only going to fail again.

"I'm sorry, sweetie," my mom said after a few moments.

"Why didn't you back me up?" I asked, pulling away from her and looking into her eyes. I wiped at my tears in an attempt to calm down.

My mother's mouth opened like she was going to

say something, but then she shut it. "I'm always here for you," she finally said. "I don't know exactly what you've seen, but I want to encourage you to go wherever your gift takes you. I don't usually get feelings about family members and people close to me, but I know that wherever you go, your abilities will keep you safe."

My tears nearly subsided in response. She was actually taking my side.

She tucked a strand of hair behind my ear. "Look, I talked to Teddy and suggested that you get some time away from the house today to think things over. I thought maybe you and Robin could go shopping or to the movies or something. He said he'd gladly take you. So, um, here are the keys to the car, and here's my credit card if you find something you think you need."

She dropped the card and keys into my hand. I met her gaze to thank her and tell her at the same time that I didn't need this. A shopping trip wasn't going to make me feel better. And then I realized something in her eyes. She was inviting me to follow my gift.

I sprang toward her and gave her a tight hug. "Thank you, Mom! Thank you so much."

"Be careful, okay?"

I nodded. "I will."

Minutes later, Robin and I were in the car. I handed him the keys.

"Your mom told me to take you wherever you wanted to go," he said.

I took a deep breath and then told him where to take

me.

12

My heart sped up before we even made it to the freeway. I was finally on my way to rescuing Hope. Well, maybe not. All I knew was that I was on my way to finding someone, whoever Penny's sister happened to be.

"So, uh," Robin started. "Where exactly are we going?"

"I already told you," I said.

"No, I know. I just mean, why so far away? I mean, there are malls and movie theaters all over the place here. Is this, like, a special mall where they have only one pair of the shoes you need in stock?"

I was momentarily taken aback. He thought I was *that* kind of girl? Not even close!

Apparently he noticed my expression. He stole a

glance at me from out of the corner of his eye, and then a sideways smile formed across his face. It was the type of smile that made my heart flutter.

Wait. What was I thinking? I forced my pulse to slow.

"I'm just kidding, Crystal. Can't you take a joke every now and then?"

I pushed a long strand of hair out of my face but didn't meet his gaze. "I guess not," I said, but what I was really thinking was that it was harder for me to take a joke from Robin than from the average person. Something about him struck a nerve every time he spoke. It was like I wanted him to think good things about me, but every joke he made just cut at my heart and made me realize that I was no different from any other girl.

He has a girlfriend, I reminded myself. And then I realized what I was thinking. I shouldn't care if he had a girlfriend or not.

"So, what exactly are we doing?" he asked again.

"Oh, uh." How did I answer this? I wasn't quick on my feet like Emma was, and when I lied, the dishonesty was written all over my face. I turned to stare out the window so he wouldn't see my eyebrow twitch, which was what happened when I lied. "Just to meet a friend." When my eyebrow didn't move, I wondered if I'd gotten better at lying or if I was putting more truth into that lie than I thought.

He didn't push the subject further, although I had

expected him to ask how I had a friend way down in Florida.

"Do you mind if I listen to some tunes?" Robin finally broke the silence that had been hanging between us for the last several minutes.

"Go ahead."

Robin connected his phone to the speakers, and an upbeat modern song began playing. I'd never heard it before. He sang along quietly. I couldn't help but notice that he had a pretty decent voice. Okay. That was a bit of an understatement. Although he was trying to stay quiet, Robin's voice filled the car with the most beautiful sound I'd ever heard. His voice somehow synced up with the singer's perfectly.

After a few songs, I found myself bobbing my head and even trying to hum along to the chorus that already played through once. I was a terrible singer, so I didn't let my voice get too loud.

Robin reached for the controls and turned the sound down until I could hardly hear it anymore. I looked up at him.

"You like it?" he asked.

I nodded. "Yeah, I really do. Who is this?"

He smiled that sideways smile again. My heart fell deep into my chest in a good way, but I quickly composed myself.

"It's Echo Score," he answered.

My face must have been plastered with a blank expression. I'd never heard of them.

His smile only spread wider. "Crystal, it's my band. Echo Score is the band I'm in."

"Oh." I didn't know what else to say. That made sense why he sounded so much like the singer. I hadn't ever realized he sang lead vocals. I always thought he sat in the background and played drums or something.

"You, uh, have a really great voice," I told him shyly, and then I turned back toward the window so he wouldn't see my cheeks flame.

"You have a gift, too," he said.

Suddenly, everything inside of my body froze. Oh. My. God. How did he know? This wasn't something I shared with a lot of people. But if he was psychic, too, then he would have picked up on it, right? Was Teddy mad enough at me to explain my gift to Robin? Would Robin actually believe me?

All these questions raced around in my mind, but all I could manage to say was, "Please don't tell anyone." The words came out sounding like I was begging him, which honestly, I kind of was.

"Why not? Your voice is great. We could use a female voice in the band."

Wait. What? "My voice?" I asked warily. So, he wasn't talking about being psychic?

"Yeah. I heard you humming over there. What did you think I meant?"

I breathed a sigh of relief then hesitated. "No, uh, that's what I thought you meant." I could feel my eyebrow twitching now, but luckily Robin was watching the road. "I just don't agree with you."

"Maybe if we put on something you know," he offered, changing the settings on the dash to play the radio.

My mouth dropped open. "You want me to *sing*?"

"Come on," he encouraged. "It will be fun. It's just us two in the car."

I stared at him in disbelief.

He looked over at me for a moment before fixing his eyes back on the road.

"You can't be serious," I objected.

"I am."

I recalled a time when Derek, Emma, and I tried to sing karaoke. Emma was the one with a voice, but we couldn't stop laughing at ourselves long enough to sing decently. I hadn't sang in front of anyone but my two best friends practically my whole life. I wasn't about to start embarrassing myself now, especially not in front of Robin.

"You'll just make fun of me, like you always do," I told him.

Robin sighed. "No, I won't. And I do not always make fun of you. I've been known to give you a few compliments every now and then. Seriously, Crystal. You need to lighten up and have some fun. You're always so serious." He poked me while he said this. Part of me wanted to retaliate and slap him in the face, but I actually found myself laughing.

The song on the radio changed. After a moment, I

noticed my favorite song was playing. It was the kind of song with an upbeat tempo that you simply couldn't listen to without dancing.

"Come on," Robin pleaded. "You have to know this song." He reached over and turned it up. He smiled and began dancing and singing in his seat. His head bobbed to the beat while one arm moved along with it.

I couldn't help it when a smiled formed across my own face while watching him. When the song hit the chorus, I reluctantly joined in. I was quiet at first and sat unmoving in my seat. Robin looked over at me, a smile still fixed on his face while he sang and danced. The look he gave encouraged me.

I closed my eyes and let my head fall back as I laughed. If Robin could act this weird in front of me, he surely wouldn't judge me to do the same. So I raised my voice and sang along. When it got to the part in the third verse where the artist was speaking instead of singing, Robin let me take it away. I even added motions and facial expressions as I sang. And then the singer belted out a really high note. I was shocked to hear the same note coming out of my own body. And it wasn't half bad!

When the song ended, Robin and I were both still laughing.

I watched him from where I sat and was completely stunned when I noticed I was having fun with him again. Robin, the guy who always had a criticism on the tip of his tongue. Robin, who I had absolutely nothing in common with except his uncle. Robin, who seemed so cool on the outside but admitted to having some dark interior I still hadn't cracked. Then again, I hadn't been worrying about the secret I was sure he was hiding because I was too worried about—

Hope. Oh, my god. How could I be having so much fun when Hope was still out there and needed my help? A wave of guilt rushed over me.

Robin was still singing along to the next song when he glanced over and noticed me looking out the window again. "Crystal, are you okay? I thought we were having fun."

"Yeah. No. I mean, it was fun. It's just . . ." I didn't know how to finish. Just then, my phone rang, saving me from an explanation. The caller ID told me it was Derek.

"Hi," I greeted. "Did you find your dog yet?"

"No," Derek said, a hint of sadness to his voice. I felt sorry for him. "That's why I'm calling. I was wondering if maybe you could . . . I don't know . . . Use your powers or something."

I remembered the way Emma and I talked about the same thing earlier, but I knew I couldn't do it. I had to have something to touch if I was going to find Derek's dog. Besides, I'd never found a living being before.

"I'm sorry, Derek. I don't think I can." I lowered my voice. "Besides, I thought you didn't even believe me." It was true. After I'd told Derek I was psychic, he'd been having a tough time accepting it as truth.

"I want to, Crystal, and right now, you're my only hope."

"Derek, I'm literally across the country. Why don't you have Emma try to find him? She's been making a lot of progress lately." I quickly realized what I was saying in front of Robin. "Just suggest it to her, okay?"

"Yeah, okay. Thanks, Crystal."

"Derek, aren't you supposed to be in class?"

He gave a bit of a laugh. "It's lunch time, Crystal." I looked at the clock. I had forgotten about the time difference. "I'll see you later, Crystal. Bye."

I hung up.

"Was that your boyfriend?" Robin asked.

"Well, he's a boy, and he's a friend," I replied.

We sat in silence most of the rest of the way there apart from me telling Robin where to go. When we drove up to the house I knew Hope was staying in, all the nerves in my body went into overdrive.

13

My palms grew clammy, and my pulse quickened. I could hardly breathe as I prepared to face the man who had haunted my dreams for weeks. And then the obvious hit me. I couldn't just walk up to his door and demand he give me Hope. Why had I even come here? Couldn't I just call the cops now that I knew where the house was?

No. I knew I couldn't do that. They would never believe in a psychic vision, and if I could somehow explain how I knew Hope was here, it would look like I was somehow involved.

"Well," Robin said. "Are you going to go meet your friend?"

My head reeled as I considered the consequences of my actions. What would happen when I went up to that door? How would I help Hope get back home? What was I even doing here? Still, we couldn't leave now. I wouldn't be able to explain what was going on to Robin, and I couldn't possibly abandon Hope.

I closed my eyes and took a deep breath. "I just need a minute, okay?"

"That nervous? Is this an old boyfriend or something?" I wasn't in the right mindset to place Robin's tone.

"No," I answered. "Nothing like that. Just a girl who used to live in my town."

But is she actually here? I wondered. The whole time we'd been driving down to Florida, I felt like I was getting closer to Hope, but now sitting in front of the house I was led to, I didn't feel her presence. And there were a lot of other things that didn't add up, like how Penny told me to help her sister, Hope, only Teddy said he knew Hope didn't have a sister, not to mention that I couldn't make sense of who would bring Hope all the way down to Florida. Could I be misinterpreting everything and headed down the wrong path once again? I shuttered at the possibility.

I needed to know if Hope Ross was in that house one way or another. If it wasn't Hope Ross, then I needed to know who else needed help and why I was sent here.

I stared at the house in front of me. It looked like a normal house, albeit small. It was a light shade of blue, complete with a small deck attached to the front and a decent sized lawn. Nothing about the house screamed danger. In fact, the house looked like a peaceful place to raise a family, but I knew that something dark lurked behind those walls.

A lump formed in my throat when I thought about knocking on the door. I swallowed to force it back down. My voice quivered when I spoke, but I didn't take my eyes off the door. "Will you come with me?" I asked Robin because I wasn't sure I could do this alone.

I knew I had to do it nonetheless. The front door called out to me, taunting me for coming this far but not having the courage to investigate. I had to do this. I had to prove to myself—and to Teddy—that my abilities were leading me down the right path, that they weren't flawed.

"Sure," Robin agreed, opening his door and stepping out of the car.

I had no choice but to follow him. My hand shook when I reached for the door handle, and I nearly missed it as my extremities came to life in a nervous shutter.

I stepped out of the car into the bright sun. My knees locked in place. Was Hope in there? Was this going to work? Why couldn't I just see the future and see what would happen if I knocked on that door? All these thoughts kept me from pushing my legs forward.

"Crystal." Robin's voice called me to attention.

I looked up at him in a daze.

"Are we going to do this or not?" Robin's eyes ran over my face, and then he stepped closer and gripped my shoulders in support. I caught a whiff of his scent and almost crumbled into his arms. His eyes were full of seriousness, an emotion I'd rarely seen in him. "Are you okay? You look pale."

I felt like I was going to hurl, but I took a deep breath instead and pushed all my nerves down my throat until they gathered at the pit of my stomach. "I'm fine," I assured him. "I'm always pale." I faked a smile to show him I was okay, but I didn't think any confidence showed through.

To my surprise, Robin grabbed my hand and led me up the walkway toward the door. I was nervous enough that Robin's touch hardly had an effect on me. I caught my breath once again as we neared the steps. When we reached the door and Robin released my hand, much of my anxiety fled away. *I can do this*, I thought. *I'm the only one who can do this.*

Robin looked at me expectantly. I raised a hand and knocked on the door. We both listened for footsteps but didn't hear any. I let out a sigh of relief, but at the same time, a wave of disappointment washed over me. I wasn't any closer to Hope than I was this morning. We waited another few long seconds. Nothing. I knocked again, louder this time.

"Sorry you came all this way," Robin said, "but I don't think your friend is home."

I wanted to be relieved since this would allow me more time to come up with a plan of attack, but I couldn't think straight. The thought of losing Hope once again consumed me. Why was I here if there was nothing to find?

"No," I insisted. "That can't be right. She has to be here somewhere."

Someone has to be here. Otherwise, why am I here? All the nerves drained out of me when I thought this, and suddenly, all I felt was a burning desire to find Hope. I gripped the door knob and twisted. It didn't budge.

I turned from the door and looked around in exasperation, hoping there would be an answer nearby. There wasn't much for activity. A few children were playing in a yard nearby, and a maroon car slowed along the street and then continued on its way. Then I noticed an elderly man sitting on a porch swing at the house next to the one I stood at. I started toward him.

"Crystal, what are you doing?" Robin asked.

Without looking back at him, I told him, "To get some answers. Just give me a minute alone, okay?"

"Okay," he agreed. His footsteps drift away as he headed back toward the car.

A faint sensation washed over me as I made my way over to the man. *Nerves, again,* I told myself.

The man smiled at me when I approached his porch steps. He was slightly plump with gray thinning hair and wrinkles around his eyes and mouth as if he smiled a lot. He was swinging back and forth on his porch swing to the rhythm of the light breeze. The air was cold against my nervous skin, which sent a chill down my spine.

"Can I help you with something?" the man asked.

I couldn't help but hold onto the porch's support beam when I made it to the top of the stairs. It was all I could do to not topple over in anticipation of answers.

"Hi," I greeted him with a smile. "Uh, my name is Crystal, and I'm just wondering if you know when your neighbors will be home. I came a long way to visit them, but they aren't there."

He looked over at the blue house. "You're looking for Lauren? She left this morning, and I haven't seen her since."

Lauren? I thought. *No, I'm not looking for Lauren. I'm looking for Hope.*

My stomach twisted at the thought of being wrong once again. How could my visions be so inaccurate? Why would I be here if the abductor didn't take Hope here? The sickening feeling returned, and I once again felt a stab of anger and frustration when it hit me that I'd made another huge mistake. I thought I had a decent grasp on my abilities, but it turns out I didn't, and that sent my self-esteem crumbling down.

I took a deep breath anyway to calm myself. I wanted desperately to be right about something. "Does Lauren have a boyfriend or something?" I asked, wondering if the abductor took Hope here at some point. Maybe Lauren was Jeff's girlfriend and he'd taken her here. Maybe she was a relative of his. "A brother or someone who has been hanging around?" I added.

The man thought about this for a second. "Not as far as I've noticed. Just her."

"What about a child?" I asked desperately. "She doesn't have a little girl with her?"

"A little girl?" The man seemed taken aback. "No. Not since . . . " He paused for a second. "No, I haven't seen a child around lately."

I thanked the man and walked back to the car. I bit the inside of my lip hard to hold back the tears and mask my utter disappointment in front of Robin.

"What was that all about?" Robin asked once I slid into the passenger seat.

"I was just asking the guy a few questions."

"What guy?" Robin craned his neck to get a good look at the house I'd just been at.

I didn't say anything. Instead, I sat there frozen, realizing what his words meant. The man I just spoke with was a ghost, and the nerves I felt when I walked up to his porch were the effects of his presence.

14

Robin suggested we get something to eat. I couldn't do anything but agree. I thought it best to have something that would settle my stomach. As we drove back to a commercial part of town to find a restaurant, I once again tried sorting through my thoughts. *Why had Penny led me here? Who was I supposed to find? Why did I find a girl named Lauren instead? Was I supposed to help Lauren in some way?* I wasn't sure I was capable of taking on another challenge since the ones I was already tackling were kicking my butt. *Why does it seem like every move I make is in the wrong direction?* I wondered.

Robin pulled into the parking lot of a small family diner and managed to find a shaded parking spot behind the building. When we entered the diner, most of the tables were empty. We slid into a booth across from each other and ordered right away.

"So, what do we do now that your friend wasn't home?" he asked. "Can you text her and see where she is? I hate to have come all this way for nothing."

Robin leaned forward across the table. His eyes bore into mine in a way I couldn't describe. It was like he was daring me to look away first. For a few moments, I completely forgot about his question and instead let myself fall into the eyes staring at me from across the table. My breath all but ceased, but my heart sped up until my fingers quivered. Without taking his eyes off me, Robin sipped on his ice water. I bit my tongue ever so slightly without realizing it.

"So?" Robin snapped me back out of my daze.

What was his question again? "What?" I asked, blinking a few times.

"I said I hate to have come all this way for nothing. Didn't she know you were coming?"

"Uh, I kind of wanted it to be a surprise."

"Can you text her, see where she is?"

"Oh, uh, yeah. Can you give me a minute?" I didn't wait for an answer. I stood up and nearly raced to the bathroom.

Once safely in a stall, I rested my head against the stall wall, closed my eyes, and took a deep breath. *I cannot be thinking about Robin right now*, I scolded myself. *Hope is my main priority. Anything regarding my abilities is my main priority.*

I took a few more calming breaths and was thankful

when I sank to the ground and the stall was big enough for me to sit cross legged in.

Hope. I need to find Hope.

As I let this desire consume me, I put all the practice Emma and I had been doing to work. I struggled to clear my mind and find something that would tell me where to go next. I only hoped it would lead me to the right place this time. Maybe Teddy was right. Maybe I was embarking on a wild goose chase.

I knew time was passing, but I didn't know how long I sat there. Gradually, I became completely oblivious to my surroundings. I wasn't in the bathroom anymore. I was floating in a different realm where I reached out to Hope. I could feel her slightly, and when I did, I pushed harder. She was lonely, but she wasn't alone. She wasn't hurt. I knew that much, and that was somewhat comforting to me. But it wasn't enough. I put every ounce of power I knew I had into connecting with her. I *had* to find her. I wouldn't accept any other alternative.

I just want to go home, Hope's thoughts said in my mind. *I want to go home where I'm with my real mommy. I want my mommy to hug me again, to call me Hope. I just want to go home.*

My eyes shot open. I was close. I was really close to Hope, but that's all I knew. I couldn't go back to Gail and Wayne's right now. I had to stick around until I knew more.

I closed my eyes again to get Hope's location, but

nothing came to me. I shook off an odd feeling as I stepped out of the stall, but I nearly jumped out of my skin when I saw a man with green eyes staring back at me. My first instinct was to scream because there was a man in the girl's bathroom, but I recognized those eyes. I quickly regained my composure and swallowed the lump in my throat. My mouth went dry, but I somehow still managed to croak out, "Scott?"

He stared back at me, and I nearly broke down. My gaze locked on his in desperation. "You have to help me! I know I'm close, but I don't know where Hope is. Why are you here? Can you tell me where she is?"

"I didn't know," he said.

Why is he here if he doesn't know where she is? I thought. *I need the answer, and being psychic isn't doing anything for me!*

Just as I opened my mouth to speak, a knock rapped on the door. My eyes darted to the door for a second then back to Scott, but he was gone. The door creaked open, and I heard Robin's voice through the crack.

"Crystal, are you okay in there?"

I couldn't answer for a moment. I didn't know how long I'd been gone. I didn't know if I *was* alright. I looked back toward the spot where Scott had been standing, but I found myself staring into thin air. "Yeah," I answered. "I'll be right out."

When I got back to our table, our food was already there. I was glad because it meant we wouldn't have to talk. My mind was still racing with questions. What was

Scott trying to tell me? What would he have said if Robin hadn't interrupted?

I was nearing the end of my meal, contemplating these ideas all the way through it, when Scott's words came back to me and I realized something. I had asked where Hope was. Scott said, "I didn't know." Not *I don't know*. I didn't know. What could that possibly mean?

As I was finishing up my meal, Robin started speaking. "So, what do you want to do now? Should we go find your friend again?"

The thought scared me. I didn't actually know where Hope was. We'd gone to the wrong house to begin with, but I knew I was close. What *could* I do now? I couldn't talk to Robin about this. He'd either think I was crazy, or if he believed me, he'd find some way to criticize how terrible a psychic I was for getting everything about Hope's abduction wrong. I thought about calling Emma and discussing the situation with her, but I didn't want to run off from Robin again. He'd know something was up, and he probably suspected something already. But I couldn't tell *him*. He wouldn't understand. Unless he was hiding an ability, too.

"I don't know yet," I answered. "Can we go somewhere to relax? Like a park or something? I just need to clear my mind."

He shrugged. "Okay."

We paid for our food and exited the diner. Robin was telling me a funny story about one of his band members while we walked. I knew he was just trying to cheer me up, and it was almost working. I had just cracked a smile when we rounded the side of the restaurant and I watched Robin's face fall. I followed his gaze and nearly crumpled to my knees. Robin rushed to the vehicle before I could truly react.

It took me a moment to digest the scene in front of me. I managed to compose myself in a brief instant and chase after him. It was all I could do not to crumble into the pit forming in my stomach.

Robin was frantic. His fingers ran viciously through his hair as he paced beside the car and cursed.

When I reached the car, I let myself finally fall to my knees. I couldn't believe what I was seeing. The tires on Teddy's car were slashed, the front window was caved in, and the passenger side window was smashed. Scratches ran up and down the side as if someone dug their key into it.

"This can't be happening," Robin said in disbelief. "Uncle Teddy is going to kill me."

It's not your fault, Robin, I wanted to say, but I couldn't move from the ball I was curled into. I stuck my face in my hands.

"What kind of person would do this?" Robin ranted. "It must have been a random hit, but why us? Why now? Why here? Teddy is going to be furious."

I squeezed my eyes shut in frustration, and then suddenly, I wasn't in the parking lot at the restaurant anymore. I found myself behind the wheel of another car. I drove along a street in a neighborhood I recognized and slowed the car as I neared a blue house. I almost pulled into the driveway until I noticed two people standing on the deck.

Who are these people, and what are they doing at my house? I thought. *I can't let them see me. Not with her.*

I sped away.

The scene shifted until a new one played in my mind. All I saw was a baseball bat connecting with the car window. In slow motion, the glass shattered in my mind.

Just like that, I was back in my own body, and I knew without a doubt that this wasn't a random hit. This was a *warning*.

15

All the stress I'd been feeling lately caught up with me in one big wave at that very moment. I couldn't breathe. Someone was out there, someone who wanted to hurt me. I gasped for breath.

"Crystal." Robin rushed to my side. Suddenly, his anxiety about telling Teddy left him and was replaced with sympathy for me.

I couldn't let Robin see me like this, but that thought only made me gasp harder. Robin's arms wrapped around me, and he pulled me into his chest. I wanted to enjoy this, to take in his scent and let his embrace envelop me in a serene encounter, but I couldn't get past the fact that someone had just vandalized our car and it was all because of me. What would they do if I pursued my visions any further?

Would they hurt me? Would someone else get hurt because of me? I trembled with fear, wondering if the perpetrator was still nearby. I couldn't help but sob into Robin's shoulders.

"Crystal, shh. It will be okay. I was overreacting. Teddy will understand."

I shook my head. Robin didn't comprehend my true fear.

"We'll figure things out, Crystal. It will be fine."

Robin pulled me in closer. I took this opportunity to bury my face in his chest. He smelled good, like a fresh spring morning. I inhaled his scent to soothe myself. He gently kissed the top of my head, and I almost pulled away in surprise, but then his arms came around me tighter, and I let myself melt into him.

When my sobs ceased, I finally pulled away. I wiped at the tears on my face. "I'm sorry," I said with a nervous giggle. "That was really embarrassing." I hated that I'd been crying so much lately.

"No," he insisted. "It's fine. I understand."

I expected him to say something witty, but he didn't. I finally nodded in agreement. Only, he didn't understand how terrible the situation truly was. What if the person who did this was still hanging around? What measures would he take the next time I tried to pursue a path in which my abilities led me? I couldn't just ignore my abilities and the messages they sent me, even if I did go on the wrong path. Would the vandal come after me?

Robin was standing up now and had his phone to his ear. My heart pounded in anticipation of Teddy's reaction.

I heard a muffled voice on the other end of the line, but for the most part, I could only hear Robin's side of the conversation.

"Uh, hi, Uncle Ted," Robin greeted nervously. He laughed, probably his way of leading Teddy into bad news. "What would you say if something bad happened to your car?" Pause. "No, I was driving safely. We're both fine. It's just . . . well, here's the thing. We went out to eat, and when we came back, your car was kind of damaged." Pause. "Well, not kind of. I mean, the tires are slashed and everything. Looks like someone thought we were an ex-boyfriend or something." Robin laughed again to ease the tension, but we both knew this wasn't a laughing matter.

I finally got to my feet while Robin spoke and walked to the front of the car to inspect the damage. That's when I saw it. I glanced over at Robin briefly, but he wasn't paying any attention to me. I reached in through the smashed passenger side window and snatched the letter from my seat. I stared at it through blurred eyes for a few moments before focusing on the words. My hands quivered, so I gripped the piece of paper with two hands to steady it.

"STAY AWAY!" was all it said, sprawled in surprisingly smooth letters.

I heard Robin's voice grow louder as he turned back

toward me. I quickly balled the note up and shoved it in my pocket, trying desperately not to let my quickened pulse show through in my expression. I couldn't let Robin believe someone had targeted us. That only meant I would have to tell him I was psychic, and I still didn't want to do that. I was sure he wouldn't believe me and would only push me away.

"No!" Robin practically shouted into the phone. "I mean, coming here doesn't really make sense. We can find someone to fix the car."

"Where exactly are you!?" I heard Teddy shout from the other end of the line.

Robin looked around nervously. "Like, four hours north or something. Look, Teddy, really, there's no reason for you to come here. That's just another eight hours of driving for you, and you'll have to get the car fixed somewhere around here anyway. We'll be fine."

My jaw nearly dropped to the pavement when Teddy agreed. When Robin finally hung up, I stared at him wide eyed. "Teddy's just going to let us handle this ourselves?" I asked.

Robin ran his fingers through his hair. "I know. I can hardly believe it either, but I guess my logic made sense to him. I don't think I could handle him seeing this. We'll have it fixed soon and be back on the road in no time."

"He didn't say anything about us being here?" At this point, I was certain he'd be more upset about me disobeying him than he would be about his car.

Robin just shrugged, which left me to believe Teddy was upset at me and Robin wasn't about to repeat what he said.

Robin searched his phone for a nearby garage and towing service. When he finally found someone, he told me they wouldn't have the right tires in until tomorrow and that we'd have to wait. Robin called a few other places nearby, but tomorrow was the best any of them could do.

I shook with nerves when Robin called Teddy back to give him the news. I was shocked when Teddy said we had no other choice but to stay the night and wait for the tires to come in. He made us promise to call the police and get a report filed before we had the car towed.

I was mostly calmed down until I saw the squad car drive into the parking lot. Luckily, the parking lot was secluded enough that we didn't have any onlookers. The note felt hot against my thigh, but I knew I couldn't tell the officer about what really happened here. My family and friends had been supportive when I found out I was psychic, but I didn't think a stranger would be. I didn't know how to explain my situation in any other way no matter how much I wanted to tell the officer this was a targeted attack.

I watched nervously as the officer stepped out of his vehicle and approached us. "Officer Brown," he introduced himself, sticking out a hand toward us. Robin shook it firmly, but I think my nerves showed through in my grip.

Robin immediately jumped into an explanation of what had happened. "We just came out of the restaurant and saw it like this. We're not even from around here. I figured it was a random hit. I've been looking around, and it doesn't look like the restaurant has any security cameras." He pointed to the areas where security cameras would be. The officer's eyes followed Robin's gaze. Mine did, too, but I didn't spot any security cameras anywhere. I was shocked that Robin was calm enough to notice this.

A sickening sensation overcame me the more I thought of the attack, which gave me a good excuse to not really pay attention to anything the officer was saying. I didn't feel like I could talk to him about what really happened, so I let Robin answer most of the questions.

Soon enough, pictures were taken and the officer had our witness report before he was on his way. I purposely left out a few details, like that I had a vague idea of who the vandal was.

Maybe I should just stop pursuing this, I thought briefly, but at the same time, I knew I couldn't just let this go.

Shortly after the police officer left, someone came to transport our car to the garage. "You two need a lift somewhere?" the guy asked. I hadn't even thought of that. What were we going to do while we waited for the car to get fixed?

"No," Robin said. "I saw a hotel down a couple of blocks. We'll stay there and then get a bus or something to bring us to the garage when you're done with it tomorrow."

A hotel? Like, I was going to be sleeping in the same room all alone with Robin? In almost any other situation, two teenagers in the same hotel room alone at night would be completely inappropriate. Then I had to remind myself that we were practically cousins. *Although not blood related*, a voice in the back of my mind—which sounded a lot like Emma's—reminded me.

Robin shared his feelings about the vandalism with me on our walk to the hotel. "Bad luck, I guess," he kept saying. We arrived at the hotel before I even realized it. It wasn't super fancy by any means, but it was a step up from the run down motel we stayed at on our way to Florida.

I briefly wondered how we were going to book a hotel room as two young teens, but somehow Robin wooed the desk attendant into letting us stay. I was grateful for my mom's credit card when I handed it over to pay for the room.

I looked around the lobby while I waited for Robin to finish talking to the desk attendant. There was an area for a continental breakfast, a sitting area with a TV mounted against the wall, and a payphone around the corner. Before I knew it, Robin was getting my attention and leading me toward our room.

"How did you do that?" I asked once we reached the second level.

"Do what?" he responded, only I heard a hint of smugness to his voice that told me he knew exactly what I was talking about.

"Get us a room. I thought you had to be at least 18 or something."

He quickly flashed me an object in his hand, but it disappeared too quickly for me to process what it was.

"Is that a . . ." I paused in realization. "You have a fake I.D.?" I hissed.

We reached our room, and Robin slid the key card in the door. "A guy can have a bit of fun, can't he?" He smiled a sideways smile before pushing into the room.

I fell onto the bed closest to the door. Everything that had happened earlier came crashing down on me all at once. Completely exhausted, I let the fatigue overcome me, and I drifted off in no time.

16

It felt like only minutes later that Robin was lightly shaking me awake, but when I opened my eyes, I noticed it was getting dark outside. I was calmed by the fact that I'd had a nightmare-free sleep but also slightly disappointed that I hadn't learned anything new to point me in the right direction.

"How was your nap?" Robin asked with a smile.

"Surprisingly good," I answered honestly. "What's up?" I sat in bed and rubbed my eyes, forcing my body to wake.

"Hear that?" Robin pressed a finger to his hear. We both paused for a moment, and I strained to hear whatever he was talking about. I did hear it. A deep bass pulsed through the walls of our hotel room.

I stared up at him. "Music. So what?"

"Not just music. A party."

I didn't take my eyes off him. "And?" I paused. Oh. "You want to go?"

He shrugged and then walked over to the other bed and sat on it. "You've just been so down lately. I've noticed you've been crying a lot."

I almost cringed at the thought that he'd noticed.

"It's just," he continued, "this is supposed to be our vacation. It's supposed to be fun. I thought it might get your mind off of things for a while."

I recalled how I had gotten my mind off things before and it led to the vision of the funeral. Maybe if I did it again, I could finally figure out the missing piece to the puzzle. But I couldn't go to a party. Apparently my expression gave away that thought.

"Come on," Robin insisted.

"Robin, look at me." I gestured toward myself. "No one is going to let me into a party." I glanced over at my reflection in the mirror on the wall. I was too skinny with small boobs and no hips to speak of. My face was that of a 12-year-old's, not a 15-year-old's, and certainly not any older.

Robin leaned across the space between the beds and gently touched a finger to my cheek. He was so close now that I could feel his breath on my face. My cheek flamed in the spot where he was touching it. He stared deep into my eyes, but I couldn't bring myself to look directly at him. I glanced anywhere but his eyes: the clock on the nightstand, the lamp in the corner of the room, and his lips. I was suddenly overcome with a desire to kiss him just to see what it would taste like. It would be my first real kiss.

My mind fought the thought as the rational part of me remembered we were almost related. But what would it be like?

"Crystal, you underestimate your beauty." That was all he said, and then he pulled away. The place on my cheek where he'd touched it grew cold in disappointment.

Why was he being so nice to me? He seemed so rude and cocky before. What had changed? I couldn't seem to sort this guy out the same way nothing else about this trip made sense in my mind. I swallowed, forcing the butterflies further down my stomach.

Robin stood and ran his hand through his hair again. "I just thought maybe you'd want to get your mind off things for a night." He shrugged again like it was no big deal, but the look on his face told me that it was.

My heart dropped. My rejection for his invitation was only breaking his heart, and I couldn't stand the thought of that. Somehow, I managed to put on a smile. "I'll go. It will be fun."

Robin beamed for a second before he realized how much emotion he was showing, and then his face fell back to its normal expression.

"Give me a minute," I told him. I dug around in my purse and found some makeup. Although I usually went light on it, I tried making it darker so I would look older. A night out with Robin could end up being really fun, I thought. Besides, what else could we accomplish by sitting in our hotel room the rest of the night?

"How do I look?" I asked, not really expecting much of a response.

Robin took me by surprise when he looked up at me. He didn't answer for several long seconds. A smile formed across his face, and then he said, "Honestly, you look really good."

My heart fluttered. That was the second time he'd called me beautiful today. It wasn't something I heard often from guys, so it immediately boosted my confidence. I pushed my hair out of my face and nervously thanked him.

While shoving my makeup back in my purse, I noticed a new notification on my phone. I quickly checked it and saw that I had a missed call from my mom along with a text.

Just checking in. Hope you two are alright.

Even without my abilities tingling my senses, I knew my mom wasn't just concerned for my physical wellbeing. She was wondering how I was doing emotionally with my gift.

I swallowed nervously, unsure of what to say to her.

We're okay, I texted. *No need to worry. Love you.*

Almost immediately, my phone vibrated in my hand.

I know, and I trust you. But I'm your mom, and it's my job to worry. Love you, too. Stay safe.

I smiled at my mom's encouragement before slipping my phone back in my purse.

"Ready?" Robin asked.

Soon, we were following the sounds of the pumping bass and I was leaving my troubles behind in the hotel room. The music grew louder as we walked. Eventually, we met up with a crowd of people swarming a grassy area. A band was playing on a stage, and some people were dancing near it. Others were seated on benches simply bobbing their heads to the beat. My confidence grew even more when I noticed that the majority of the audience was teenagers.

A gate lined the perimeter of the park. A few people stood near the entrance in matching red t-shirts that read "Autumn Fest Battle of the Bands." Their shirts had the dates of the competition on them, and I noticed the event lasted all week—every night through Thanksgiving. We paid our admission fee and entered the premises to explore. Food vendors sat along the peripheral of the lot along with booths housing band tees and CDs.

I almost smiled when I caught Robin bobbing his head out of the corner of my eye.

"These guys are pretty good," he said. "Almost as good as Echo Score."

I was about to ask him who Echo Score was before I remembered that it was his band. *Almost as good*, I thought. *Of course he would say something like that.* I listened to the music coming out of the speakers, and I decided that he was right. Echo Score *was* better.

"What do we do now?" I asked.

"What?" he shouted over the music while moving his body to the beat.

I leaned into him so he could hear. I could feel heat radiating off his body and was suddenly overcome with a desire to touch him, but I resisted. "What do we do now?" I repeated loudly.

Robin smiled that sideways smile that made my heart do flips. "We dance!"

I wanted to pull away from him and refuse his offer when he grabbed my hand and pulled me toward the stage. His touch sent an electric current through my hand and toward the rest of my body. Suddenly, I didn't want to let go. I couldn't do anything but follow him.

A voice in the back of my mind scolded me. What was I doing thinking about Robin like that? I didn't like him, and we were going to be related soon. Shouldn't this be weirder than it is? Besides, what would happen if it didn't work out between us? Every Thanksgiving and Christmas would be super awkward once Mom and Teddy got married.

Robin and I reached the space in front of the stage that people were using as a dance floor. The beat was great, and I chuckled when Robin swung his body to the beat. It wasn't exactly spectacular dancing, but I could see his confidence shine through, which made him look even better at it. I'd never really danced much before. I didn't know how. I smiled up nervously at him, half enjoying his outgoing nature and half trying to reassure myself that a night away from my worries was what I needed.

Robin leaned in close to shout in my ear. "What's wrong?" His hot breath touched my skin, melting my insides.

"I don't know how to dance," I admitted.

He rolled his eyes at me, not in a condescending manner, but in amusement. "It's easy. Just jump up and down. Sway your hips."

I glanced around nervously and watched the girls around me for inspiration. I awkwardly tried to sway my body in the right direction, but it felt too weird.

Suddenly, Robin's hands were gripping my hips and guiding them. "Like this," he said, but I could barely hear him or the music over my own pulse pumping loudly in my ears. For a second, it felt like my heart was floating in my chest as it flipped anxiously. Then it was back, pounding against my rib cage.

I couldn't take my eyes off Robin until he released me. I caught a glimpse of a circle of teens behind him who were jumping up and down to the music. I figured that was the best way to dance without embarrassing myself, so that's what I did. Robin didn't jump along with me, just sort of banged his head to the beat and added arm motions that surprisingly didn't look half bad. As Robin and I moved more, I became more confident in my dancing. I was actually having fun! I jumped and giggled, and he stared back at me. The song ended then, and I stopped, unsure of what to do next.

"See? You're having fun, aren't you?" Robin asked.

"Yeah," I admitted. "This was a really good idea."

The band on stage said a few words and then began playing their next song. It was a slow, romantic song in complete contrast to their last one. People began moving off the dance floor, thinning the crowd. The few who stayed grabbed a partner and swayed slowly in a circle. I looked around nervously. *What do I do next?*

I was about to find a bench to sit on when Robin's hands settled on my waist. My breath caught, and I looked up at him in shock. Something about his expression sent my body immediately melting into the situation. I reached up slowly to test his reaction and then wrapped my arms around his neck. Should I be doing this? His hands gripped tighter around my waist, and he pulled me in. I briefly wondered what his girlfriend would think of this, but I couldn't think far enough past his touch to worry too much about it. Besides, I knew I didn't have a shot with him. I was practically his cousin, and I was too young for him anyway.

I blinked a few times, wondering what I was doing. When Robin's arms held me in an embrace, I took it as in invitation to rest my head on his chest. I could smell the fresh spring scent again, and it made every sensor in my body come to life. I didn't want the song to end.

What am I doing here? I thought. *How did I go from hating Robin so much to being filled with this desire to never let him go?* I shuffled through my memories of the past few days. *When did things change?* I remembered when he opened up to me and told me he was insecure. He hadn't been mean to me since. Did that conversation perhaps mean a lot more to him than I thought it did?

Actually, I recalled, he'd been nice to me since I made us chase after the wrong guy. Was he taking pity on me for embarrassing myself, or did he actually admire me for following my intuition like he said he did?

My head spun along with our movements as we slowly shifted to the melody. I closed my eyes to relish in the glory of his sweet embrace. When I opened them, I wasn't on the dance floor anymore.

17

Green eyes stared back at me. I wanted to move in surprise, but my body stayed put, fixed on the green eyes peering up from behind the sink I was standing next to. I pushed myself away from the countertop, and so did the man I recognized as Scott, only he looked younger. I wanted to open my mouth to ask him why he was here, but my body wasn't moving on my own accord. When each step Scott made mirrored my own, I realized I *was* Scott and that he was looking in a mirror. I had somehow stepped into one of Scott's memories.

I—or rather, Scott—finished washing my hands and turned to the paper towel dispenser. The Crystal part of me could feel the discomfort of being in someone else's body. It wasn't quite the same as when I had visions while I was asleep. I was more aware of things now, like that I was actually Crystal and this wasn't real. At the same time, I struggled to pinpoint my own thoughts while experiencing Scott's memory. I took in what I could about the situation. Scott looked younger than he had when I met him. He was wearing a Florida University hoodie, so I figured I was in a memory from when he went to college. But *why*?

Scott exited the bathroom, and I heard music booming down the hall of the campus building. He showed his student I.D. to the attendants at the door where the music was echoing into the hallway. Scott's memory told me he was joining an end-of-semester party hosted on campus. The attendant stamped his hand before he entered the vast room. The music grew louder, and almost immediately, his body began rocking out to the beat. His eyes scanned the dance floor and struggled to make out each figure. He was looking for someone, but the Crystal part of me didn't know who.

His gaze locked on a woman who was facing away from him near the middle of the dance floor. In his memory, everything else around her faded — the lights, the music, the room — until it was just a woman with red curly hair dancing alone. When Scott began pushing through the crowd and making his way toward her, the music and lights returned to his memory.

"There you are," he said once he reached the girl.

She turned, her beautiful red curls flying around her face gracefully. My heart nearly dropped out of my chest when I—Crystal—realized that I recognized the girl. Who could miss red fiery hair like that? I knew I had seen her at Scott's funeral.

The memory continued, even though I had no idea what it meant.

The girl beamed up at him. "Scott. You made it!"

He smiled back at her. "I wouldn't miss it for the world."

She reached for him and pulled him into a hug. He never pulled away from her but rather wrapped his hands around her waist.

"I was really hoping you'd make it tonight so we could talk later," she shouted over the music.

"Oh? What do you want to talk about?"

The girl wouldn't meet his eyes. "I think it's best if we talk about it later. Not here."

Scott put a hand to her face and guided her green eyes back to his. "Look, I'm sorry I'm leaving, but my family needs me back home." The words should have come out quietly, but Scott couldn't tell her how sorry he was with his tone over the pumping bass. "Dad's sick, and Mom can't handle it alone. We all know Jeff isn't going to help. My parents don't even want him around anyway after all the crap he's pulled. Let's just enjoy our last night together. How does that sound, Lauren?"

Shock riveted through my conscious mind.

Lauren smiled back at him, and then Scott pulled her in closer and slowly brought his lips to hers.

The scene shifted around me. I felt woozy for a second, and then my sense of balance returned. But something was different. There were still lips locked on mine. I opened my eyes to see Robin's face not even inches from my own. And then the realization of what was happening hit me. I was *kissing* Robin. His lips were soft on mine, and I couldn't help but go faint at the encounter. He tasted *so* good.

Suddenly, the rational part of my mind broke through the confusion. I found enough strength to push away. All I could do was stare at him in shock. Did I just have my first kiss? My first kiss was the result of a ghostly encounter? That just didn't seem right.

"What?" Robin asked, stepping closer to me.

I took a step back.

"What's wrong, Crystal? It wasn't good?"

It took me a few seconds to process his words. Hold on. Was he saying he was kissing me back? But what about his girlfriend? My head couldn't take all the confusion right now. I had visions and pieces of the puzzle to sort through. I had to figure out why Robin was kissing me. Did he *want* to kiss me?

I couldn't breathe. I gasped for air.

Robin immediately rushed to my side. "Crystal, are you okay? What's wrong?"

I blinked a few times, trying to regain my strength. "I just—I want to go back to the hotel," I managed to say, although my head was spinning so fast that I could hardly understand him. My balance seemed slightly off, and I wasn't entirely sure if it was because I'd just had a vision or if it was some reaction to my first kiss. I didn't have time to decide the cause of it. I gripped Robin's arm for support and waited until my sense of balance returned.

"Crystal, are you sure you're okay?"

"I am. I just think I'm getting sick." My eyebrow didn't even twitch when I said this, which told me that I believed my own words. "I don't mean because of you. Sorry. I just . . . Can we please go back?"

Robin led me back to our room, insisting that he support me the whole way so I wouldn't pass out. I assured him several times that I was fine, and he finally quieted.

Once things went silent on our walk back, I attempted to sort through what I knew. Scott knew a woman named Lauren. That just happened to be the name of the woman's house Penny sent me to. Lauren was at Scott's funeral just before Hope was taken. Scott went to school somewhere down here, which is where he met Lauren, which would mean that Lauren was probably from around here. That's why Hope was here. *Because Lauren was the abductor.*

My mouth literally dropped open when this hit me. I know I should have had a much different reaction, but I couldn't help it when a giant smile came to form across my face. I wasn't wrong! I was actually getting somewhere. My abilities weren't failing me. Suddenly, I felt a restored level of faith in myself. I knew what I had to do. I had to go to sleep and hope that my dreams would tell me where Lauren and Hope were, not to mention that it would help if I knew *why* Lauren took Hope.

Although I'd napped not long ago, I fell asleep almost instantly when we returned to the room.

I woke to the feeling of a hand gripping hard around my mouth. Like every night I encountered this, I wanted to scream, but nothing came out. The Crystal part of me that was watching the scene through Hope's eyes struggled to think straight. *I am not Hope*, I told myself. *I am not being abducted. Think. What's here that you've never seen before?*

Even as I thought this, my mind was still caught in confusion. A part of me felt like I was Hope, yet I still knew I was Crystal. The Crystal part of me fought to push through the barrier that muddled everything. I needed to let go of Hope's fears and think objectively. I needed the Crystal part of me to *see* something. I pushed harder. *Come on.* Suddenly, the Crystal part of me broke through.

And then it hit me. Just like that, the obvious washed over me, and what I hadn't ever seen before— what Hope hadn't seen that night—became crystal clear. A red curl peeked out from behind the assailant's hood. I always thought the perpetrator was male, but now that I looked closer, I realized that the figure was slim.

Suddenly, a lot more about what had happened

made sense, like how when I'd tried connecting with Hope, I felt like she didn't like her *new* mommy.

Hold on, Hope, I said in my mind. *I'm coming for you.*

Once the car door slammed shut and I saw Hope's freckles and big chocolate eyes in the car mirror, the scene shifted around me as if someone smeared paint across a canvas only to uncover another image underneath.

I stood in a room filled with chairs with an aisle running down the middle. A casket sat at the front of the room, and a photograph of Scott stared back at me. I was back at his funeral. *But what am I doing here?* I thought. I spun around the room to take in my surroundings.

A strange feeling once again called to me from the back of the room. My eyes followed the source, and they fell upon Jeff. Next to him sat a woman with a fiery red bun and black hat.

I drew in a sharp breath. *Lauren.*

Her eyes were fixed on something the same way Jeff's were when I first encountered this scenario. I followed her gaze to the front of the room. Hope was in her same chair, fidgeting the same way she had the first time I saw her in this same scene. Jeff wasn't the only one watching her.

My heart beat wildly against my chest as all the pieces of the puzzle began falling into place. *But why? Why had she taken her? Were Jeff and Lauren working together? Where is Hope right now?*

Before I had a chance to draw in another breath, the scene shifted around me once again. I heard the beeping of the machines before my eyes adjusted. A white curtain separated the room I was in, and voices whispered behind it.

"You'll be okay, honey. I promise," a woman said. I recognized Lauren's voice.

I took a step closer to the curtain. For a moment, I was afraid she would catch me spying on her, but then I remembered I was seeing into the past. It was always easier to recognize a vision when I wasn't seeing it through someone else's eyes.

I crept around the corner of the curtain in the hospital room to view the scene. Lauren sat next to the bed and had her hands wrapped around those of a little girl's. For a second, I thought I saw Hope lying there, but then I realize that this girl was older and had lighter eyes.

Penny.

Of course! I thought. I remembered something Penny had said to me. *I don't think she's safe. My mom has kind of . . . gone crazy. She's not herself.* I scolded myself for not seeing the connection sooner.

"I'm scared, Mama," Penny said from the hospital bed. Tears rose to her eyes, which only made my heart sting. The way mother and daughter looked at each other was almost too sad to bear. I knew how this story ended. I knew Penny wasn't going to make it.

"Honey, the doctors perform surgeries every day,"

Lauren assured her. "They know what they're doing."

Penny sniffled. "I just . . ." She trailed off, unsure of what to say.

Lauren ran a hand through Penny's brown hair. "You've had heart surgery before, and look how strong you came through. We can't accept anything less than you making it through this time." I had a suspicion that Lauren was saying these words more for her own sake than for Penny's.

"Colette and Abby will be here in the morning to wish you good luck," Lauren told her. Fear held strong in her eyes when she stared at her daughter.

I couldn't take it anymore. Even though Lauren had taken Hope, I felt bad that she'd lost Penny. A sob caught in my throat the same time I was whisked away from the dream.

I sprung straight up in bed. My sheets were damp with sweat, and my mind was reeling. It took a few seconds for my eyes to focus, and when they did, I found two figures standing at the end of my hotel bed.

18

"You have to help her," Penny pleaded.

My hand came up to support my pounding headache. It was early, so little light was seeping in through the windows. I looked back and forth between the two figures. Scott and Penny stood at the foot of my bed, side by side. Their eyes were the same color of green, and their facial features were strikingly similar. How could I not have noticed this before? Everything was starting to make sense now. I was overcome with relief knowing that I wasn't wrong about everything and that my abilities were still leading me in the right direction.

"You didn't know," I whispered so quietly that even if he was awake, Robin wouldn't have heard me.

They both looked back at me with a quizzical

expression.

"That's what you said to me," I explained to Scott. I heard a stir from the other bed and looked over at Robin. He was still asleep, but I lowered my voice anyway. "I thought you misspoke when I asked you where Hope was. You said, 'I didn't know.' You meant you didn't know about Penny, didn't you?"

I could see it in his eyes. That's what Lauren wanted to tell him that night they were dancing together. That's what he never knew.

"Look," Scott said. "Lauren isn't dangerous. She's just . . . not herself. You need to get Hope back to her mom for everyone's sake. Lauren needs help."

Everything was making sense to me now, but I still had so many questions. Why did Lauren take Hope in the first place? Why didn't anyone suspect her? Where was Hope now?

"Where is she?" I asked, but before I could get an answer, both figures disappeared the same moment a voice cut through the momentary silence.

"Who are you talking to?"

My head jerked toward Robin in surprise. My heart sped up, and my breathing quickened. I'd just been caught, and I couldn't meet his gaze. "Um . . . myself," was all I could say. I could already feel my eyebrow twitching before I said it.

Robin narrowed his eyes at me. It was that same look everyone else gave me when I told them I was psychic, like they didn't quite believe me.

I could feel my face flush. I wasn't sure if it was because I'd been caught talking to ghosts or because seeing him made me think about our kiss last night.

"You were talking to yourself?" Robin asked skeptically.

I still couldn't meet his gaze. Since I'd learned about my powers, I'd been wary about telling anyone. My mother warned me about telling people, but as my eyes lifted to meet Robin's stare, I saw a glimmer of something in them. For a moment, I thought he might actually believe me. I again wondered if Robin had a gift like Teddy did, a heightened intuition. If he did, I couldn't pass up a chance to share this with someone my own age.

I sighed, preparing myself to divulge my secret. It felt like the right thing to do. "Okay," I started slowly. "I wasn't talking to myself. I was . . ." I didn't know if I could say it, yet Robin had been so nice to me after I thought I saw the abductor in the gas station. Maybe he had realized I was psychic and took a liking to me because of it. I wrung my hands in my lap. It all made sense, so he'd have to believe me, right?

I took another deep breath and forced down any uncertainties I had about telling him. "I was talking to a ghost," I told him slowly. "Well, two, actually." I couldn't look at him when I said this. I was always afraid of people's reactions after I told them. For some reason, though, telling Robin brought even more fear and nerves to my body. In all fairness, I didn't know him that well. I used that as justification for why I was feeling so weird telling him my secret.

I waited for what seemed like forever, but it must have only been a split second. Robin didn't react the way I thought he would. I was expecting one of two things. Either he would excitedly admit he was psychic, too, or he would scoff and make fun of me. Either way, I would know if he was psychic or not.

But neither of those things happened. He just sat in his bed and looked at me expressionless. It was impossible to tell what he was thinking.

"Robin?" I finally broke the silence.

His expression shifted. My heart sank deep into my chest when he said, "Are you trying to tell me our hotel room is haunted? I'm not going to fall for that."

I held my breath in an attempt to think straight. What did that even mean? Was he saying he didn't believe me?

"Robin," I scolded. "Be serious for a second. I'm trying to tell you a very important secret, and it's really hard for me." I forced myself to meet his gaze to gauge his reaction.

A smile formed across his face, and for a second, I thought this was it. I thought that he was going to tell me he was psychic. Instead, he just sarcastically said, "Yeah, okay."

"Wait, you mean, you're not psychic?" I thought I had put the pieces together and that I had figured him out. I could feel he had a secret, and being psychic seemed logical seeing as Teddy had some sort of gift, too.

He laughed. A hole formed at the pit of my stomach, and my eyes burned. I couldn't believe I'd just divulged my deepest secret to someone who didn't understand. Mom had told me people would use it against me. She had warned me about telling too many people. Suddenly, Robin felt like one too many, and that made my heart ache on a deeper level than I thought possible.

Disappointment washed over me when I realized my suspicions about him were completely off. If he wasn't psychic, then what secret was he hiding? I asked the question in my mind, and suddenly, the answer came to me. Certain things about him started making sense, like how he always wore long pants, how he wouldn't go swimming with me or touch the water on the beach, and how he wouldn't jump up and down at the concert. That's why he'd scowled at me when I ran around the motel and made fun of me because I played sports. It's why he wanted to go into occupational therapy.

"I am psychic!" I insisted. I couldn't stand the thought of him not believing me. He just had to. "I'll prove it. If I'm not psychic, how do I know about your prosthetic leg?"

Robin recoiled in shock.

"Your 'defense mechanism?' You're self-conscious because of your leg."

139

Anger flickered across Robin's face, but then his expression shifted. "That doesn't prove anything."

"How else would I have known?" I challenged.

"My uncle," he said as if the answer was obvious. And it was. Why hadn't the universe given me something good to convince him with?

"Let's stop playing games," Robin insisted. "I know you're just trying to get out of talking about what happened last night."

I was momentarily confused, thinking he was talking about my vision on the dance floor, but how could he know about that? An instant later, the rest came back to me.

"Oh. Right. Our kiss." I could hardly say the words myself, as if saying it was admitting it happened. My voice came out as a whisper. "I'm sorry about that. I, uh, wasn't myself."

"Sorry? Crystal, if I remember right, I was the one who kissed you."

19

I gaped at him for a second before composing myself. I had assumed the kiss was my body acting on the motion in the vision. Nothing about this seemed to make sense right now.

Most of all, I couldn't figure out why he would kiss me. Especially not when he had a . . . I interrupted my own thoughts so I could speak. "But, you have a girlfriend! I won't help you cheat on someone."

His brow furrowed in confusion. "A girlfriend? Where'd you get that idea?"

"That girl you're always texting. I asked you if she was your girlfriend, and you said she was."

Robin looked confused for a moment and then threw his head back and laughed. "Sage? I may have said something, but I never said she was my girlfriend.

You assumed that all by yourself. She's just my lab partner. We were talking about our homework project. And I wasn't just texting *her*."

Something about this newfound knowledge left me with a sense of relief. It meant that Robin was available that we could . . . Wait. "But we're, like, cousins," I pointed out.

Robin shifted and came to sit on the edge of his bed just a few feet from my own. His body was so close to mine now, and it felt like as each second passed, he closed the gap another inch. He was still wearing his jeans, but he didn't have a shirt on. I couldn't help but notice the fantastic curves of his abs. I looked away quickly before he would notice, and I discovered I was biting my lip. I stopped instantly.

"Crystal, it's not like it's incest. We're not actually cousins." The way he said it sounded like an invitation, which only made my desire to touch his polished skin burn brighter.

"And what if it doesn't work out?" I asked. "Wouldn't things be weird between us?"

Robin shrugged. "And what if it does work out? You wouldn't want to miss that chance, would you?"

Silence stretched between us as if the questions didn't actually need answering.

"So, what?" I finally asked in a quiet voice. "You like me?" I couldn't believe I was asking him that, nor could I contain my heart in anticipation of his response.

He smiled that sideways smile that made me go

faint. I longed to kiss him again. "What's not to like? You have a strong personality, you're a lot of fun to be around, and you're really pretty."

I could hardly focus on his words. All I could pay attention to right now was his fingers caressing my face when he said I was pretty.

"Plus, I really feel like I can talk to you," Robin said. "All that stuff I said on the beach—about my insecurities. I wouldn't admit that to just anyone. I haven't been able to stop thinking about you since. About . . . doing this."

The next few moments passed in slow motion. My heart thumped quicker in my chest, yet the sound of my pulse slowed in my ears as if time altogether decelerated. Robin's hands came to cradle my face as he leaned across the space between the beds and pressed his lips to mine. I met his lips in return. I was too overcome with a need for him to even wonder if I was doing it right.

The last few moments disappeared to the back of my mind as a greater sensation overcame me. I completely forgot my anxiety about telling him my secret. His reaction didn't even register in my mind as my lips crushed into his for a second time.

His hand moved into my hair and then trailed across the back of my neck. His tongue lightly grazed my lips. I wanted to grab and claw at him and press my body tight against his.

Instead, I pulled away. Part of my mind scolded my

actions, but I thanked another for being rational. We both breathed deeply as we came up for air. I couldn't help but marvel at Robin's smile, and when I couldn't take it anymore, my face broke into a full on grin. I'd never imagined a first kiss—or rather, a second kiss— would feel like that. But as much as I didn't want it to ever end, it didn't feel right with everything else happening right now that needed my immediate attention.

I didn't have to say anything. Robin nodded his head in understanding. "Thank you," he said.

"For what?"

"Pulling me off of you."

I laughed.

"I mean, Uncle Teddy and your mom trust us. It just wouldn't be right to do it here."

My eyes widened.

He caught a glimpse of my face and quickly corrected himself. "No! I didn't mean that! I respect you. I mean . . . Let's just take it easy."

A part of me didn't want to. A part of me wanted to jump on him and lock my lips to his and never stop. But I knew exactly what he was saying.

"It's just that I really like you is all I'm saying," Robin explained.

My heart fluttered at the compliment, but I also knew I needed to put some distance between us. He was right. It wouldn't be right to break Mom and Teddy's trust.

DESIRE in FROST

"Well, uh, I'm going to go to the bathroom," I announced, my anxiety showing through in my tone.

Once I had a chance to get away from him for a few moments, Robin suddenly became less important in my mind. I desperately wanted him to believe me, but the fact that he still liked me even if he didn't accept my abilities left me with a sense of comfort.

Still, I had bigger things on my plate. I hopped in the shower and let the mystery of Hope's abduction consume me. Now I had most of the pieces to the puzzle, although it should have been obvious to begin with. I still had one problem, though. I had to rescue Hope. But what could I do? Lauren already knew my face. She knew what car we drove. She would never open the door to us. Besides, what would happen if she *did*? How would that actually help anyone?

When I exited the shower and was pulling on my clothes from the day before, a knock sounded at the bathroom door. "Do you want to go downstairs to get some breakfast?" Robin asked through the door.

"Why don't you go on without me? I'll be down in a few minutes."

I heard the door to our room click behind him. I quickly reached into my purse and grabbed a handful of change and turned to make my way down to the lobby.

Just then, my phone rang. The caller I.D. said it was Emma, so I answered right away. "Hello?"

"Hey, Crystal. Are you ready for our yoga session? I texted you but you haven't answered yet."

I pulled my phone away from my face. Sure enough, there was a message notification. "Sorry. There's just been a lot going on lately. I don't think I can join you this morning."

"Why not?" Emma's voice filled with disappointment.

"I don't have my computer with me, so we can't video chat."

"Use your phone," Emma suggested.

"Now's not a good time," I admitted. "My yoga mat isn't even here."

"What? Where are you?"

I wanted to tell Emma about Robin so badly, but I knew she'd just rub it in my face that she was right. My heart flipped at the thought as I replayed Robin's kiss in my mind. I was glad she was right, yet I had so much more to tell her. "Well, uh, how much time do you have?"

"I still have time before I have to leave for school."

Right. It was only Wednesday, so classes were still going on.

Emma's tone shifted and rose a few notes. "Are there juicy details?"

I couldn't help but smile. *Yes!* I wanted to shout, but I kept my cool. "Well, let's just say you were right about Robin."

Her voice rose about two octaves as she squealed into the receiver. I had to pull the phone away from my ear to avoid hearing loss. I could feel my face flame in response to her excitement.

"What happened?" Emma asked once she calmed herself down. "And where are you?"

"We kind of got stuck in a hotel room together," I confessed.

"Like, overnight? Did anything happen?" I could practically hear her raising her eyebrows suggestively through the phone.

The idea of teasing her with fake juicy details crossed my mind, but I was too excited about what *did* happen between us that I told Emma the truth.

There was a brief silence, and in that moment, I remembered the change in my hand. I knew there were more important matters to attend to than spilling details about my love life, no matter how much I wanted to talk about it.

"Speaking about love," Emma started, but I cut her off.

"Look, Emma, I have to go. I'll tell you everything later about me and Robin and everything else that's happened, okay?"

"Okay, I guess." Disappointment held heavy in her voice. "Well, have fun! Bye."

I hung up the phone and plugged it in to charge—luckily I had my charger in my purse—before leaving the hotel room. When I reached the first floor, I hung around the corner near the payphone and peeked toward the breakfast area to check on Robin. He was facing away from me and trying to choose a muffin flavor.

I turned toward the payphone and slipped a quarter in. I didn't know if I actually needed one to dial 911, but I put it in anyway. When a voice picked up on the other end, I lowered my tone and gave her Lauren's address and told her that's where Hope Ross was.

"Can you please tell me your name?" the woman on the other end of the line asked.

I hesitated. I couldn't. They'd ask too many questions, and they wouldn't believe me. I hung up. Just because I was paranoid, I used the bottom of my shirt to wipe the phone of any prints, even though they didn't have my prints on file and that didn't make a whole lot of sense.

My heart beat wildly against the walls of my chest at the same time I breathed a sigh of relief. This was all over for me now. The police would find Hope, Lauren would get the mental help she needed, and Penny and Scott could cross over.

My nerves eased, and I smiled as I basked in the glory of completing another psychic mission. I finally rounded the corner to meet Robin for breakfast. Now that I knew Hope would be safe, I let myself focus on Robin. I filled my plate with free food—they even had bagels, my favorite—and went back to sit by him. He smiled across the table at me, and I couldn't help but get lost in his eyes.

I took a gamble and asked him about his leg about halfway through our breakfast. "So, what happened?"

Robin shifted, and I could tell the subject was uncomfortable for him.

"I'm sorry. I didn't mean to prod or anything. I'm just curious."

"No, it's okay," he assured me. "It was a bad car accident a couple of years ago. All I lost was a leg. It could have been worse."

All he lost was a leg? He seemed a little too optimistic about the situation, but something about his positive attitude made me like him a little bit more.

"And you can still drive?" I asked.

"Oh, sure. No problem."

I wasn't sure how much the subject bothered him, so I dropped it, and we talked about happier things like his music. He told me a little more about his friends who were in his band, and I shared a few of the less embarrassing stories about Emma, Derek, and me. We went back and forth like this for what seemed like hours but probably wasn't. I laughed at his stories and was honestly enjoying myself.

In the middle of our lighthearted chat, a strange but all too familiar sensation suddenly overcame me. My joy came to a screeching halt when I looked up and saw a girl with dark brown hair and green eyes standing at the other end of the room. Penny stared back at me with an expression that told me this wasn't over yet.

20

I excused myself and dropped my paper plate in the trashcan Penny was standing next to.

"What is it?" I hissed more sharply than I intended. I was sure this was all over and Hope would be returned safely home, but the look in Penny's eyes told me I wasn't even close to done with this mission.

"They're gone!"

"What?" I kept my voice low and glanced around to make sure no one heard me. Robin was rising from his chair and would be next to me in a matter of moments. I threw Penny a glance to make it quick.

"They're not at my house anymore. You still have to find her."

I could feel Robin's heat radiating off his body as he came in close to me, almost touching, and threw his own dishes in the garbage.

"Ready?" Robin asked.

I wanted to smile up at him and never let go of the mood I was in just moments ago, but the high I was feeling plummeted to the ground as I processed what Penny had said. I didn't think about what I was doing when I wrapped my arms around Robin's waist and rested my head on his chest. I just needed a bit of emotional support. His fresh spring scent soothed me.

"You okay?" Robin asked, running a hand through my hair.

I pulled away from him and forced a smile onto my face. "Yeah, I'm fine." I turned away quickly when my eyebrow started twitching.

We spent the next few hours in our hotel room listening to music until the garage called and told us our car was ready for pick up.

I tried my best not to worry about Hope in those few hours. Part of me was really enjoying Robin's company and wanted to bask in the glory of it. Another part of me trusted that wherever Lauren took Hope, the police would use my anonymous tip and somehow track them down. I also reminded myself that I still didn't know where Hope was and that the best thing I could do was forget about her and enjoy myself so that another vision would come and show me where to find her. Yet my heart knotted while I guiltily enjoyed myself instead of focusing on Hope.

The hotel graciously let us ride their shuttle to the

garage. When we got there, the car looked good as new apart from the few scratches that remained. It was hard to believe that just yesterday the tires were slashed and the windows were smashed.

Soon enough, we were on the road. Being in the car again only made me think back to what the vehicle looked like the day before when we walked out of the restaurant. I remembered the note still shoved in my pocket. I couldn't look at it, but it made me think of how serious Lauren was about Hope. I still didn't quite understand what drove her to take her away from her mother. In fact, there were a lot of things I still didn't understand, but I knew there was nothing I could do about it right now. I'd already tipped off the cops, and that was the best solution I could think of.

The series of events that had transpired over the last few days once again ran through my mind, and I thought back to when I had tried to tell Robin I was psychic, only he didn't believe me. But he still liked me. I didn't get it, but I knew that above all else, I wanted — no, I needed — him to believe me.

My hands knotted in my lap, trying to work up the courage to talk about it. I'd only told people close to me, people who had known me for years. None of them seemed to flat out reject the idea as much as Robin had, yet right now, he was the one I wanted to believe me the most.

For the longest time, I didn't think I could bring up the subject again. To ease my shaky hands, I knew I needed to give them something to do, so I dug my phone out of my purse and texted Emma. I noticed she'd already left me a text asking about the details between Robin and me, so I told her as much as I could. I wasn't expecting her to respond because I knew she was in class, but she must have snuck her phone in because she texted me back right away. *Sounds romantic!*

Yeah, but there's more, I texted back. And then I went on to tell her as much as I could through text about what had happened with Hope over the past few days. *But Robin doesn't believe me*, I complained. *I really want him to.*

Have you told him about Hope?

Not yet.

Well, maybe you should.

I really wanted to take Emma's advice, but it was hard enough for me to tell him in the first place. I didn't want to get rejected again, especially now that I knew he didn't share my gift in any capacity.

Did you find Derek's dog? I asked when Emma didn't text for a while.

Not yet, she texted back with a sad face.

Are you using your, I paused typing, trying to come up with the right word, *abilities?*

I've already told you I don't have psychometry.

But you get feelings. Go around town and see which direction feels right, I suggested. *Maybe get Sophie and Diane to help.*

That's a good point. Now go convince Robin what you can do.

I smiled at Emma's last text. It was so like her. I sat

in my seat quietly for several long minutes, stealing glances Robin's way to try gauging what would convince him. I rolled my owl necklace between my fingers for good luck and took a deep breath. I opened my mouth to cut through the music playing in the car, but my jaw snapped tight before I could get a sound out. I must have done this two or three more times as I contemplated what to say to him, until I finally managed to squeak out his name.

Robin looked at me and turned the radio down. "Something bothering you?" His eyes shifted between me and the road.

My gaze fell to my hands. "I'm fine." I didn't even bother hiding my twitching face this time. The lie showed through in my tone.

Robin glanced at me again and then turned his eyes back to the road. "No, you're not. Is it about us? Because we don't have to kiss again if it's too weird."

"No!" I practically shouted. I didn't want to think about ending things with him, even though we weren't anything official yet.

"I mean, it's not that. It's . . ." I didn't speak for several long seconds, and Robin let me have a moment to collect my thoughts. "It's about what I told you earlier. I know you think I'm crazy, but it's the truth."

A look of confusion fell over Robin's face like he didn't know what I was talking about. "Oh," he finally said. "You mean about the hotel being haunted?"

"Robin, I'm serious. I never said the hotel was

haunted. I said that I saw ghosts. They aren't attached to the hotel. They're attached to . . . me, I guess."

When Robin didn't say anything, I continued. "They came to me for help. The girl I went to meet, she's not exactly my friend. I wasn't lying when I said she was from my town. It's just that she's six years old. Her sister and dad came to me asking me to help her because she was abducted."

I waited for Robin's response. Yet again, he didn't react how I expected him to. I was sure he would cut me off at some point and tell me I was crazy, but he didn't. He simply narrowed his eyes in thought while I spoke. I gave him a few moments to digest this, and then his words cut through the silence.

"Crystal, I can tell that you believe every word you're saying." His tone had a hint of something to it I couldn't quite pinpoint.

"What do you mean by that?" My voice came off sounding more offended and accusatory than I intended.

He sighed and glanced at me. "I mean I can tell when you're lying. Your eyebrow twitches every time you do."

My hand flew up to my face. "What? It does . . ." I trailed off. I couldn't even try lying about that now. How did he know? Did Emma tell him?

"I noticed," he said, answering my unspoken question. It only made me blush at the realization of how much he'd been paying attention to me.

"Well, then you should know I'm not lying about being psychic," I insisted.

"Like I said, I think you believe it. It's not hard to lie about something you believe as truth. But how am I supposed to believe in something like that?"

His words cut deep, but I still understood on some level where he was coming from. *Now, how do I convince him?*

"The car," I blurted without really thinking about where I was going with this.

Robin shot me a confused expression.

"It wasn't a random hit," I explained. "I knew when it happened that it wasn't. It was Lauren."

His blank expression reminded me that he didn't yet know who Lauren was. I quickly told him everything I knew about the case before he could interrupt me. When I recounted the part about the car, even though he clearly knew this part, I finally told him about the note left in the passenger seat. I dug into my jeans pocket and pulled it out.

"And how do I know you didn't write that yourself?" he asked skeptically.

I looked at him in disbelief for a few moments. "Robin, look at the handwriting. You've seen my handwriting. I write in chicken scratches. You know I can't write this well."

He took a long look at the paper before turning his eyes back to the road. Then he glanced at me a few more times. "You are serious, aren't you?"

I breathed a sigh of relief. "That's what I've been telling you this whole time!"

"Well, that explains a lot, I guess." He paused, and I could tell he had more to say, so I didn't interrupt him despite the anticipation that was killing me. "Okay," he said. "I believe you. But you know what that means?"

"What?" I asked, a little afraid of the answer at the same time my heart flipped.

"It means we're going to have to find that little girl with or without Teddy's help."

I beamed. Robin was on my side.

21

When we made it back to Wayne and Gail's and entered the front door, everyone flooded us with questions.

"Are you two okay?" my mom and Gail said at the same time.

"How's the car?" Teddy asked.

"What exactly happened?" said Wayne.

Robin and I both exchanged a glance because we didn't know which question to answer first. After a moment of silence, Teddy stood from the couch and asked Robin to show him the car. Teddy stuck his hands in his pockets and remained surprisingly calm. He followed Robin outside, leaving me to answer everyone else's questions. I quickly peeked out the front window. Teddy was assessing damages and running a finger along one of the scratches that the garage hadn't buffed out.

I answered everyone's questions the best I could without revealing to Wayne and Gail why Robin and I were there in the first place. I assured them we were both alright, and eventually, they were satisfied with my answers.

I stole another glance out the front window. Teddy had his arms folded across his chest and was leaning against the vehicle, staring seriously at Robin. I couldn't tell what they were discussing, but I thought I saw a hint of a smile cross Robin's face.

I excused myself and exited to the back porch so I could put on some clean clothes. A quiet knock came at the door just as I was slipping on a fresh t-shirt. "Come in."

"Sweetie," my mom said kindly, poking her head onto the enclosed porch. She slowly moved her way into the room and then closed the door behind her.

I smiled to let her know I was fine, but I wasn't sure the smile reached my eyes. "Yeah?"

She reached out to me and pulled me close. It felt good to be in my mother's arms. She was warm and familiar, and for a second, it felt like the events of the past few days hadn't happened. Then she pulled away and broke the spell that made me forget about my troubles.

"How'd it go?" she asked. Even though she never explicitly admitted to helping me out, I could tell by her tone that she was wondering about Hope.

"Not well," I admitted. "I learned a lot more about things, but she's still missing." And then I explained to my mom everything I knew so far. I excitedly told her that she was right about there being something more to my dream that I needed to pay attention to, but then my voice fell flat in disappointment when I recounted the rest of the story.

We were seated side by side on the air mattress, which needed pumping up again, when she wrapped a single arm around me. "You'll find her. I know you will."

I smiled at her encouragement. "I hope so. I just wish the answers came easier, you know?"

"Just give it time. Be patient. I'm sure things will work out."

I wanted to believe her, but every step I took toward Hope seemed to push her further away from my grasp. I wanted Penny or Scott to show up again and to just give me all the answers, but I already knew it had been tough for them to show themselves to me in the first place. Maybe we could hold a séance. It had worked for us in the past, but the more I thought about it, the more I figured it probably wouldn't work with just two people. I decided to take my mom's advice and be patient. That's what seemed to be working best for me lately.

"Did anything else happen on your trip?" she asked.

"No, not real — what?" I cut off.

My mother raised her eyebrows and twisted her lips up.

"What?" I asked again. Heat rose to my cheeks.

"You think I can't see what's going on?" she asked. I could tell by the look she was giving me that she knew exactly what was going on, but how?

"I thought you didn't get feelings about your family members," I pointed out.

"Sweetie, this is not a psychic feeling. It's a mother's intuition. I saw the way you looked at him when you two came in the door."

I wasn't about to lie to my mother. I didn't even have a desire to lie. A smile formed across my face, and I could feel the blood rise in my cheeks. "I know it's kind of weird with you and Teddy getting married and all, but I really like Robin."

"Did you two . . ." Her voice trailed off.

It took me a few seconds to realize where she was going. I recoiled in shock. "What? No! Robin's not like that," I told her. "And neither am I," I added. "It was just a kiss. Or two. But Mom, it was my first kiss!" My body shivered with excitement. I knew some girls wouldn't be comfortable telling their mothers this, but my mom was different. She was like a best friend to me.

She smiled back. "As long as you're happy."

I returned her smile. "I am."

Silence stretched between us for a few long moments until I finally broke it. "You don't think it's

161

weird, do you?"

"Why would it be?"

"Well, because after you and Teddy get married, we'll kind of be cousins."

My mom laughed. "I guess so, but I think you two are mature enough to make your own decisions."

She quickly kissed me on the side of the head and left the room. I was sure she intended to leave at that moment to let the statement sink in. She always did that. I took a few seconds to really think about it, and I decided I was proud my mom thought I was mature.

Robin entered the porch a few minutes later while I was pumping up the air mattress. "So, uh, everyone done freaking out?"

I chuckled. A joke like one he would make in this situation danced on the tip of my tongue, but I couldn't quite think of the right way to word it, so instead I just said, "Yeah. I seemed to convince them we were fine." When he didn't say anything, I spoke again. "So, how'd it go with Teddy? Was he really mad?"

Robin stared at me seriously. "I think that if he wasn't a cop, he probably would have murdered me on the front lawn."

My eyes widened. "He's that mad?"

Robin laughed, and my body relaxed. "Nah, I'm just kidding. He took it surprisingly well. I think he's just glad we're safe."

"Did he get mad about us taking the trip even though he didn't know about it?"

"We didn't really talk much about that."

"Oh," I said flatly. "What did you talk about?" I pushed down on the mattress to test its firmness and then turned off the air pump.

Robin sat on the mattress and shrugged his shoulders casually. "You."

"What?" I squeaked. I swallowed, returning my voice to normal. "Only good things, I imagine."

That sideways smile that made my heart flutter crept across Robin's face. "I told him about what a terrible, horrible person you are." His tone didn't reflect his words, and he still had a smile fixed on his face when he slowly leaned in toward me.

My heart thumped. Oh, my god. Was he coming in for a kiss? My brain could hardly process what was going on as a fire rose within my chest and spread out through my face and my extremities. Robin paused just inches from my face, his gaze seductively shifting between my lips and my eyes. I hardly noticed when my lower lip curled into my mouth and my teeth came to clamp down around it.

"Food!" Gail shouted from the kitchen, pulling me out of my trance. Apparently Robin felt the same way because, like me, he instantly recoiled.

I finally had a chance to catch my breath and realized what was just about to happen. Then Robin's fingers grazed over mine and held onto them for a moment until he rose and walked out of the room. He looked back at me for a second before leaving.

Something gleamed in his eyes, and he raised his brows a bit. I silently cursed at him when I realized he was teasing me the whole time. I wanted now more than ever to kiss him. Instead, I was forced to follow him out into the kitchen and try not to let the thought of him overcome me during our meal.

The rest of the day I spent purposely getting my mind off Hope, waiting patiently for something to come to me. A part of me felt guilty for not worrying about her, but another part of me knew that I'd done all I could up to this point. Yet another part of me wanted to be consumed by thoughts of Robin. We didn't get another chance alone since Mom, Gail, and I spent time chatting and playing cards while Robin, Teddy, and Wayne enjoyed their own guy talk in the living room.

I fell asleep that night dreaming of Robin. In my dream, Emma and I were singing as part of his band. There was another girl there, too, someone who my mind told me I was friends with but, when I woke up, I was sure I'd never seen before. It was a comforting dream that made me feel like I could be a real part of Robin's life.

22

I woke Thanksgiving morning feeling utterly guilty. No visions of Hope surfaced in my dreams. I still didn't know where she was, and I wasn't sure if my anonymous tip led to her safety.

After showering and getting dressed, I found my way into the living room. Everyone was awake except Robin. He was stretched out across the pullout couch shirtless. My eyes lingered, and I consciously let them stay fixed to his abs. I nearly drooled at the sight of him.

After several long moments, I snapped myself out of it and reminded myself why I came in here in the first place. I didn't want to wake him, but I turned the TV on anyway and kept the volume low. I sat in the chair on the other side of the room and flipped through channels until I found the news. My eyes fixed on the screen for several long minutes without hearing a single thing about Hope. I wasn't sure if that confirmed anything or not. I didn't know how far the news would travel or which stations would pick it up.

Robin's voice pulled me from the TV. "Hey," he greeted in a tired tone.

I smiled wide at him without trying to. "Good morning."

He looked at the TV and didn't say anything, but I could tell he knew why I was watching it. He smiled back at me. "Good morning to you, too." He yawned and stretched his arms above his head.

My eyes danced around his chest again, but they lingered a bit too long when he came down from his yawn and noticed me staring. His smile spread wide as if he was teasing me. I blushed. I was grateful that Teddy walked into the room just then to keep Robin from saying something that would make me turn pure crimson.

"Put some clothes on," Teddy teased, tossing one of the throw pillows at Robin. It hit him in the face, but he just laughed and pitched it back. I was glad they were getting along and that Teddy wasn't too upset about everything.

Robin groaned at the thought of getting out of bed, but he finally stood, grabbed a shirt that was slung over the side of the couch, and walked out of the room toward the bathroom as he slipped the shirt over his head.

"Does he sleep with his leg?" I asked absentmindedly.

Teddy rolled his eyes. "He probably shouldn't, but he's self-conscious about it. I'm surprised he even told you. He gets upset when anyone even mentions it, and he made half his family promise not to tell anyone else. I can't say I understand why, though maybe he doesn't want people to take pity on him."

I shrugged nonchalantly.

Teddy took a seat at the end of the pull-out bed and stared at the TV for several long seconds. The look in his eyes told me he wanted to say something more. I did him a favor and broke the silence first.

"Look, Teddy," I started.

He tore his gaze from the TV and stared at me. He offered a half a smile that told me he was sorry for the other day. I was happy to have the old Teddy back. My hand clamped around my owl pendant, the one he had given me, in hopes of finding a bit more courage to speak to him about everything that had happened recently.

"I'm really sorry about running off like that," I said, staring down at my hands. "She was there. She really was, but now she's not, and I don't know where Lauren has taken her." After I said it, I almost expected him to ask who Lauren was, but then I figured my mom passed on the information I had told her.

"I'm really sorry I didn't believe you," he admitted. "I just," he cleared his throat, "just wanted to let you

167

know that my team is looking into things further now. We've notified the larger departments we've been working with and labeled it an anonymous tip. No clue as to where she's taken Hope, though." He wouldn't meet my gaze when he apologized. "I just want to thank you for your help."

"Teddy, did Mom tell you I called in an anonymous tip? You should probably get in contact with the area police department to see what they've found. Maybe they found something at the house."

Teddy nodded. "I'll look into it, Kiddo." He stood and exited the room.

My heart softened. Teddy was starting to trust me again, and that filled me with more confidence than I'd had this whole trip.

Almost immediately, Robin reentered the living room freshly dressed. "What was that about?"

"What? Oh, Teddy. He was just apologizing."

"Yeah, I told him to," Robin said casually while he cleaned up his blankets and folded the bed away.

"What do you mean?" I sat up a little straighter in my chair.

Robin shrugged. "I just think that if he asked for your help, he shouldn't have been so quick to dismiss it, so I kind of scolded him and told him to apologize."

"You scolded him?" I raised my eyebrows.

He nodded as he moved about the room. "I kind of have that effect on my uncle."

I gave a light chuckle, but Robin's words had me

wondering. Was it because of Robin that Teddy was putting a bit more trust into me again? I had no doubt my mom talked to him, too. Even if I didn't have Teddy's full trust, I did have my mom and Robin on my side. Realizing this made me feel like all my troubles and responsibilities with my gift were vanishing, if only for a moment.

For most of the rest of the day, I helped my mom and Gail in the kitchen. They put me in charge of the apple pie. My mom joked that since it wasn't a salty dish, there was no fear of me over salting it. I joked back and told Gail to put my mom in charge of the salad so she couldn't burn anything.

My mind wandered back to Hope every so often, praying that the police would find her. There simply wasn't anything more I could do at this point.

Just as I finished washing my hands after cutting apples, my phone rang. I quickly dried my hands and answered Emma's call.

"Hello?" I quietly excused myself from the kitchen and entered the enclosed porch for a bit of privacy.

"Hi, Crystal! How's your Thanksgiving going?"

"It's okay. We're just cooking and watching the Macy's Thanksgiving Day Parade. You?"

"Well, with my parents' divorce, things are kind of weird. Mom was going to cook, but my dad thought he deserved to have me for the holidays since, you know, I live with my mom. So I just said screw it to both of them, and I'm having dinner with Derek's family. His twin sisters are so cute!"

I felt a stab of emotion—one I couldn't quite pinpoint—when I thought about her and Derek hanging out and having fun without me. I wished for a second that I could be there with my two best friends.

"I can't believe you ditched your parents like that," I told her, but the truth was that it was something I could totally see Emma doing. She was always more bold than I ever was, and with her parents going through a divorce, they were both probably quick to give her whatever she wanted.

"Eh, I couldn't take their bickering," Emma continued. "Someone has to show them that there are consequences to fighting. But that's not why I called. I have some great news!"

Emma paused, and I knew she was waiting for my response, so I played along and prompted her. "What is it?"

"I found Derek's dog!" She screamed with excitement.

"That's great!"

"I did just what you said. Derek and I walked around town, and I could just *tell* when things felt right and when they didn't. We ended up finding Milo across town. This little kid, like 10 years old, convinced his parents to take him in. Since he didn't have a collar on, they didn't know what else to do. But Milo was excited to see Derek, so it wasn't hard to convince the kid that Milo was Derek's dog."

When Emma found out I was psychic, my mom told her that normal people can have mild psychic abilities if they work hard enough at them. For a long time, I thought maybe she was crazy. I didn't think Emma would develop psychic powers, but the truth was that Emma put a lot of work and practice into strengthening her intuition, and she was getting really good at it. So when Emma told me her news, I smiled, honestly happy with her progress.

"That's really cool to hear. When I get back, we should do some more practice together."

"Yeah, I'd like that," Emma agreed.

Emma and I talked for another few minutes, and I filled her in on the latest details of Hope. I wanted to talk with Emma longer and maybe even get some insight from her, but after a while, she told me she had to go. I could hear laughter in the background and again thought about how I missed my friends.

When I stepped out of my guest room and saw Robin across the kitchen, though, my mood lifted. I only hoped that after this trip was over, he would somehow find a place in my group of friends so I wouldn't have to choose between them.

Robin laughed at something Gail said, and then his gaze met mine. His smile touched his eyes and somehow found its way into my heart and made me beam back at him. I joined my family in the kitchen, and Robin and I finished preparing the apple pie together as we all talked and laughed.

Eventually, we gathered around the table and said grace. Robin's chair was pushed so close to mine that I could feel the heat radiating off his body. It was driving me nuts, and I could tell by the sideway glances and smirk he was throwing me that he knew it. He was such a tease.

"Andrea, Crystal," Gail addressed my mother and me. "There's a little tradition our family does every year at Thanksgiving. During our meal, we go around the table and say one thing we're thankful for. I'll start it off this year." Gail's eyes trailed around the table at each of our faces. "I'm thankful you were all able to make it this Thanksgiving, and I'm thankful I got to meet you two," she said, looking from my mother to me. "I'm very happy for Teddy and glad to hear about the engagement." She smiled. "I know that was more than one thing, but I have so much to be thankful for."

It was Teddy's turn next. His eyes fell on my mother, and he had that same expression as the night he proposed. "I couldn't be more thankful that Andrea said yes to my proposal."

My mother smiled and kissed Teddy lightly on the lips. Then it was her turn. She looked at me. "I'm thankful that my daughter has grown into a strong young woman."

I blinked in shock. I knew my mom was proud of me, but I was sure she would say something about Teddy before she'd say something about me. Something about her words and the way she looked at me held a deeper meaning. I was pretty sure she was telling me she was proud of my abilities. I was trying to figure out what exactly she meant that I missed what Wayne had said. I may not have heard Robin if he hadn't said my name.

"I'm thankful for Crystal," he said, looking at me.

Wait. What?

I could feel my face flaming. Out of all the things in the world that he could be thankful for — that he survived the accident that took his leg or that he had an amazing singing voice and a band to help express that — he chose to be thankful for me. My pulse quickened, and I blushed in flattery.

Something in Robin's eyes held a hint of romance, the same type of look Teddy had just given my mother. From under the table, he took my hand and squeezed it tight. My stomach flipped in response.

"I know we only just got to know each other," he said, "but I'm thankful we had the chance to."

For a moment, it seemed like we were the only two people in the world. Everything else in the room faded into nonexistence until the only thing in my vision was Robin's face. Then I suddenly became aware of all the eyes staring at us. A part of me shivered with nerves, especially because Robin and I would be step-cousins in a few months and I still found that a little weird. But when all I saw were smiles staring back at me, I realized the happiness on everyone's faces doubled as a look of approval.

I beamed back at Robin. "I'm thankful for you, too."

"Your turn," Gail told me.

"I just went. I said I was thankful for Robin."

"You can't choose the same thing as him," she teased.

My mind raced. There were many more things I felt ungrateful for than those I felt grateful for. If they asked me to spout off that list, I could do it in a heartbeat. I was ungrateful for the fact that I still hadn't found Hope. I was ungrateful for the feelings of guilt and disappointment that the situation brought me. I was ungrateful that no matter how many questions I asked regarding my powers, only more inquiries arose. I was ungrateful that I had to keep it such a secret—something that I tried to do for my mother's sake since she'd warned me to keep it quiet.

But another part of me had so much to be thankful for, like the way my gift brought my mom and me closer together since we shared it, or the way it made me feel like I had a sense of purpose bigger than myself. Or how I could tell my friends about my gift and no one had pushed me away because of it.

All these ideas went through my head in a split second, and then I knew what to say. "I'm thankful for my talents and abilities." Little did Wayne and Gail understand just exactly what I was capable of.

Dinner seemed to end too soon, and I'd shoved myself so full of stuffing and potatoes that I didn't have any room left for desert. Everyone else apparently felt the same way. Wayne suggested that we wait an hour or two before dessert, and we all agreed that was a good idea.

"Want to take a walk down to the water with me?" Robin asked.

I was more than happy to accept his offer despite feeling like I could hardly move. His fingers intertwined with mine, and he led me down the staircase to the sand. I could hardly stand up straight as my body came alive with butterflies. We sat next to the water with my hand still in his.

"So," I started. Robin's eyes met mine, and the glow of the setting sun only enhanced his blue irises. I tucked a loose strand of blonde hair behind my ear. "What are we exactly? Am I, like, your girlfriend?"

Robin chuckled. "If you want to put a label on it."

"I don't mean to pressure you," I cut him off. "I mean, we don't need labels if you don't want them."

"No," Robin said. "I think it's good. I'd like to be someone's boyfriend for once."

I stared back at him, hardly able to believe what that statement meant, like he hadn't had many girlfriends before. I was too afraid to ask about that, though. I just smiled instead, happy to realize that one issue seemed to be resolved. But something in my face must have given away my anxiety about other issues, yet Robin didn't seem to read my expression correctly.

"You don't want labels?" Robin asked.

ALICIA RADES

"No. I mean, yes. Yes, I do. That's not the problem."

"Oh? What is?"

"It's just . . ." I stared down at the sand, attempting to pick out patterns in it. "It's nothing about you. I'm really nervous about Hope. I haven't heard anything, and I'm still afraid for her, you know?"

My eyes were still locked on the sand when Robin spoke. "Maybe this will help ease your nerves." And then he pulled me in close and touched his soft lips to mine. The kiss wasn't too soft, but it wasn't smothering, either. His lips parted ever so slightly, and his tongue grazed against my lower lip. My hand came up to cradle his face as his lips crushed into mine. A feeling of warmth consumed my chest, making me want to melt into the sand below me. I became so lost in Robin's touch that for those few moments, everything seemed to disappear except for him.

Eventually, we both pulled away. It was silent for a long time until I finally spoke. "Why are you thankful for me?" I blurted. I immediately wanted to take it back, but the question was already out in the open.

"What do you mean?" Robin asked.

"I—uh . . . Nothing. Forget about it."

"No," Robin insisted, but his voice was still soft and kind. "Tell me."

"At dinner you said you were thankful for me. There are so many other things you can be thankful for. Why me? I mean, if we're being honest, we still hardly know each other."

"Hardly know each other? Crystal, I've been able to open up to you more than I have to anyone in practically my whole life. Shutting people out, it's what I do, but not with you. These past few days, you've made me feel like I finally have someone I can share myself with. And what about you? How many people have you told about your abilities?"

I mentally ticked off the people in my head. I'd told Mom and Teddy, and of course both Emma and Derek knew. Justine and Kelli only knew because I'd used my powers to rescue Kelli from an abusive relationship, and Justine was helping me. And then there was Sophie and Diane, Mom's business partners who were also psychic. I reviewed the list in my head and realized that all these people had one thing in common: I trusted them. And now there was Robin, and I'd told him, so that must have meant I trusted him.

"See?" Robin asked rhetorically. "I opened up to you. You opened up to me. It's not something I experience often, and I kind of like being able to talk to at least one person. *That's* why I'm thankful for you."

"Oh," was all I could say because his answer was so simple. It made complete sense. "Well, there's still a lot I don't know about you, like what your favorite color is or what your relationship is like with your parents or what your friends are like."

Robin thought about this for a moment. "You know the real me, and that's what matters." For a second, I thought he was going to leave it at that as he put an arm around me and pulled me closer, but then he continued speaking. "But just so you know, my favorite color is blue, my parents and I don't spend a lot of time together—my dad is kind of a hard ass—but we get along, and my best friends are basically idiots." He rolled his eyes and laughed at his last comment.

He went on to tell me about his friends, and we ended up talking until after dark about the simple things in life. I nearly forgot all my troubles.

Eventually, my eyes began drooping, and I took in a deep yawn.

"Tired?" Robin asked. "Am I boring you that badly?"

"No!" I nearly shouted because he wasn't. Then I looked at him and realized he was just teasing.

Robin and I walked back to the house together and went our separate ways.

When I crawled into bed that night, I fell asleep almost immediately. That night, I dreamt about Hope's abduction again, only this time, I saw it from a different angle.

23

Lauren's thoughts played in my mind.

I didn't plan this. It's not something I came to Minnesota to do. All I wanted was to pay my respects to the father of my child. I wasn't even supposed to be here. It was practically sheer luck that the obituary made its rounds on social media and far enough through my connections that I even heard about Scott's death. I wasn't invited to the funeral, but I found my way in anyway. I hid myself in the back of the room where the family wouldn't notice me.

Only after I sat down did I realize the guy I'd sat next to was Scott's brother, Jeff. I wasn't quite sure because I'd never met him, but he fit the description. I noticed he was sitting alone, which made sense based on everything Scott had told me over the years. I shifted nervously at first, but if Jeff was anything like Scott talked about him years ago, then he wasn't exactly on speaking terms with the rest of the family, so I knew he wouldn't rat me out, not that he had any idea who I was.

I tried not to cry during the funeral. I'd done enough crying over the past few months. But then I saw her.

Penny, I thought.

Somewhere in the back of my mind, a voice was telling me that the little girl sitting at the front of the room wasn't my daughter, but I couldn't fight the feeling that she needed me just as much as Penny did. And I had failed Penny.

Was this the second chance I'd been praying for?

The little girl turned around in her seat. I caught a glimpse of her profile, and my breath caught in my throat. Her eyes were darker than Penny's, a deep chocolate brown instead of hazel. Her hair was shorter, too, but it fell to her shoulders in the same shade that Penny's did. Those freckles. I could swear they were set in the exact same pattern as Penny's were.

I couldn't help but watch her while the funeral service continued. Tears pricked at my eyes when I thought about Scott's death, but they started falling — and I quickly dashed them away — when I saw the little girl who reminded me so much of my own daughter. When the service was over, my eyes were still fixed on her. I noticed the woman she'd been sitting next to was talking with a few other guests. She didn't even acknowledge the little girl.

I could do so much better, I thought. This time, I won't let Penny die.

The thought only crossed my mind for a second. I knew there was something off about the idea, but I still couldn't take my eyes off the little girl. The more I looked at her, the more she morphed into Penny in my mind. Penny had been gone for so long. All I knew was that I had to get her back and keep her safe this time. Something shifted inside of me – something I couldn't quite pinpoint – when I made this decision. Penny was always at the forefront of my mind, but now she became the sole focus of everything that I almost forgot why I was here.

When I found myself parked in front of a house I didn't recognize, I was dazed. It was dark outside, so I knew time had passed since the funeral, but I couldn't place where I'd been or what had happened in the past few hours. I didn't know how I got there or what I was doing. I looked around frantically as my body adjusted to the situation. I knew I was sitting in my own vehicle. The driver's seat was familiar, and the moon glowed off the maroon hood.

I looked further past my vehicle and noticed that I was in a residential area, but I didn't recognize the place. My eyes fixed upon the house I was parked in front of. It had orange lights strung around the doorway and lit jack-o-lanterns on the stoop. It didn't look familiar in the slightest. I took in the details of all the other houses along the street. At first, my gaze shifted past the house across the street, but then I noticed a black vehicle sitting in the driveway. I knew I'd seen it before, but I wasn't sure where. A quick memory flashed back in my mind, and a little part of me knew I'd followed it here.

I continued to eye the house and wondered why I was here. That's when I saw her again. The young girl passed in front of the window, and my breath all but ceased.

"Penny," I said out loud.

I opened my car door and stood on the pavement. When I looked back, I saw a woman pass by the window, too. She never noticed me sitting outside her house.

I can't go in there now, *I thought.*

I sat back in my car, wondering what I was going to do to save my little girl. I had to get Penny back. She'd been away for so long. Is that why I was here? To get my daughter back? It felt too much like fate to turn back now.

The air was chill in the car after opening the door. I grabbed my hoodie from beside me on the seat and slipped it on. I didn't know exactly what I was doing. I wasn't even thinking. I stayed in the car for another hour watching the house. The light in the living room turned off, and another one flipped on at the other side of the house. I watched the woman pass by the window a few times in her nightgown, and then she shut the light off again.

I waited another hour to make sure she was asleep. I knew I had to get to Penny as soon as I could, but if I was going to get away with her and bring her back home to Florida, I had to be patient.

I flipped my hood up when I got out of the car to shield my body from the chilly night air. The sleeves fell to my fingertips, so I balled them into my fists. I walked around the corner of the house and peeked in the windows. It wasn't easy to see inside, but there was enough moonlight that I could make out each room.

I stopped when I came across a room I was sure was Penny's. A nightlight enveloped the room in a soft hue. The walls were pink, and there was a collection of teddy bears in one corner.

Of course, *I thought*. Penny always loved her teddy bears.

I noticed a small lump on the bed.

Penny! *I almost shouted, but I kept my mouth shut.*

I pressed my cloaked hands against the window and stared into the room. All I knew was that I had to get to her, but I wasn't completely sure how. I could try the front door. I could break the window.

I pushed away from the glass in exasperation, and to my surprise, the window moved. It was only so slightly, but it was enough to tell me that it wasn't locked. I had found my way to Penny. I fit through the window easily. For a moment, I just looked around the room again, and then I stared at the girl.

What am I doing? *a voice in the back of my mind asked. But then I looked at her face. I really looked at it, and I knew she needed me. Knowing there was another woman in the next room, I figured it best not make any noise.*

A moment later, I had my hand clamped down around Penny's mouth. I pressed a finger to my lips to let her know to be quiet. I knew she would. After all, she was my little girl. *I hugged her close to me, and she wrapped her arms around my neck. I finally had my little girl back.*

I crawled back through the window I came in from and used one hand — still shoved in my hoodie for warmth — to pull it down and press it shut. I set Penny in the passenger seat of my vehicle and then crossed around to my side of the car. I was so happy to have my daughter back.

My dream appeared to fast forward though the events of the next few weeks, and I caught glimpses of

Lauren and Hope in my mind. The images slowed when Hope asked to play at the park and Lauren reluctantly agreed. A few hours passed through my mind in a second and then slowed again when I saw myself through Lauren's eyes standing on her front deck. Days flew by in a few short moments, and then the images regressed to normal speed and fell upon a yellow house just as small as Lauren's.

***

I sat up straight in bed and gasped for air. I was partially relieved to know why Lauren took Hope and that it wasn't in malice that she did so. I knew she hadn't, and didn't intend to, hurt her. Most of my relief, however, came from the fact that I now knew where Lauren took Hope. I didn't know who the yellow house belonged to, but I somehow knew this was where Lauren took Hope after she destroyed our car.

Light gently seeped in the porch windows, and I could hear voices in the kitchen. I leapt from my bed and excitedly entered the kitchen. "Teddy," I practically shouted.

He looked up expectantly from the newspaper he was reading.

My eyes shifted from Teddy to my mom and then to Gail, who was tending to breakfast by the stove. "Can I, uh, talk to you two in private?" I asked, looking between my mom and Teddy.

They exchanged a glance and then rose from the table and followed me onto the porch that served as my guest room. "Did you find out anything about Hope?" I asked Teddy once my mom shut the door behind us.

Teddy's face fell. "I'm sorry, Crystal. We haven't found anything more, but it turns out that Lauren was a good lead. After getting her description out, some witnesses recalled seeing her at the funeral. She wasn't on the guest list, and Melinda didn't remember seeing her, which is why we didn't know to look into her to begin with," he explained. "There wasn't anything else to connect her to this initially. She hadn't been in contact with Scott for years. The problem is that the local police have searched her house but didn't find anything. There's no indication of where she took Hope or if she's hurting her or anything. There haven't been any reports matching her license plate number, either."

"That's great!" I said, but I didn't mean it in that way. Both my mom and Teddy fixed a look of confusion on their faces. "I mean, I know where she is now. I don't know how, but I do. And it's on our way home!"

Like the last time, I couldn't pinpoint an address. I had to physically go there if I was to find it.

"We have to go get her," I told them. "I mean, we're headed home today anyway." I wanted to hate Lauren for taking Hope, but a part of me felt her pain. "And we have to help Lauren," I added.

24

I never knew how I knew it, but I was able to tell Teddy where to go. Within a few hours, we were pulling up in front of a small yellow house along a one-way street.

Who lives here? I wondered. *And why would Lauren bring Hope here?*

Teddy stopped the car in front of the house but on the opposite side of the street. He looked back at me from the driver's seat. "Remember, we do this my way. Andrea and I will ask questions. You stay here."

I knew Teddy had already mentioned this, but my jaw still dropped in disbelief. My mother got to go with him, but I didn't? But this was *my* responsibility. *I* was the one who was supposed to rescue Hope. My heart dropped knowing I wasn't going to be a part of it, but the rational part of me was just glad Hope would be safe whether I was in the midst of the action or not. Teddy gave me a serious look, and I quickly agreed that I would stay put.

"I hope you have your hand cuffs," I said before he exited the car. I was only half joking, but he shot back a knowing smile that told me that he had them on him. I didn't even know if he could arrest someone here, but that didn't matter to me when Hope needed rescuing.

Teddy and my mom exited the car together. I glanced over at Robin. His eyes were closed, and his chest rose and fell slowly. I almost thought about waking him and telling him we were here, but he looked so peaceful. I didn't want to disturb him.

I watched out Robin's window and hardly noticed I was holding my breath as Teddy knocked on the door. It felt like time stood still, waiting for something to happen. Teddy pounded on the door again. The anticipation was killing me, but after several long minutes — or at least what felt like it — the door swung open, and a woman with dark hair and olive skin stood behind it. She must have been in her 30s, but I didn't recognize a thing about her. I didn't know what I was expecting — maybe Lauren or someone who looked enough like her to be her relative, or perhaps a male who could have been her boyfriend — but when I caught a glimpse of the woman, the pieces of the puzzle just didn't fit right.

My heart sank in my chest. Was this another mistake? Why was it that every time I felt close to Hope, something happened that only pushed me further away? I was sure Teddy was going to be furious that I'd led him on the wrong path again. Never again would I hear him say he trusted my judgement.

Just as I watched Teddy flash his badge, my phone vibrated in my pocket. I didn't want to respond, but the vibrations continued. The only person who ever called me was Emma, so I answered it.

"Hello?" I answered quietly, careful not to wake Robin. My gaze never shifted from the front door of the yellow house.

"Crystal," Emma breathed a sigh of relief as if she had been holding her breath. Something in her tone hinted at urgency, leaving my body frozen in fear.

"Emma, are you okay?"

"Yeah, I'm okay. Are *you*?"

"What do you mean? Of course I'm okay. Why do you sound so terrified?"

"I just—I guess it's nothing. I just got a really bad feeling. I wanted to make sure you were okay."

"A bad feeling? About me?"

"Yeah. You're not near a white garage, are you?"

"What?" I didn't quite understand where she was going with this. I glanced up and down the street. The houses were all so colorful here. "No, no white garage."

"Good. I'm just getting a bad feeling about a white garage. Just don't go into it, okay?"

"Uh . . . okay. I don't imagine that I will, but thanks for the warning." My eyes stayed locked on the woman's porch. She stepped out onto it and closed the door behind her. I saw lips moving but didn't know what they were saying—probably Teddy just asking routine questions. I needed to pay closer attention. I needed to know what was going on, to see if there was any hint in the woman's words that told me why I was sent here. "I have to go, Emma. I'm kind of in the middle of something really important."

"Okay. Just be careful."

"I'll be fine, Emma. You don't have to worry about me."

We said goodbye and hung up. I really wanted to know what was happening on the porch. I slowly climbed over the middle console and crawled into the passenger seat. I knew my mom had an extra key to Teddy's car, so I quickly dug it out of her purse and stuck the key in the ignition just enough to roll my window down a crack in hopes of making out some of the conversation on the porch.

When I turned back to look at the house, I saw it. The corner of a white garage peeked out from the side of the yellow house. It was tucked far back from the street, but it was the only white garage I noticed. I could hear the voices on the porch now, but I couldn't make out what they were saying. My pulse quickened, and my eyes locked on the white building situated behind the woman's house.

Emma knew it was going to be there. She warned me about it. That meant it was important somehow. And I knew exactly how. Hope was in that garage. Those long moments the woman took getting to the door must have been spent sneaking Hope out of the house. I may not have believed it myself if I didn't feel it in my bones. I knew Hope was close, and something about the garage called out to me.

I didn't process what I was doing when I slid out of the vehicle. The promise I'd just made to Emma moments before didn't even register in my mind while I moved. Teddy's and my mom's eyes were on the woman while her own gaze stared in the opposite direction down the street from me. Nobody saw me slink around the side of the house next door and double back through that person's back yard. I couldn't explain what possessed me to sneak to the garage on my own. It was as if my abilities were drawing me in and the rational part of me all but ceased to exist.

I stayed low as I approached a window on the side of the garage. My heart pounded against my chest in preparation to face the unknown. I pressed my back against the side of the garage and peeked into the window. For a brief moment, everything within my body froze. A small figure was curled up in a chair near the far side of the garage. Her knees were pulled to her chest and held tightly by her arms.

My nervous system went into overdrive. I recoiled from the window and rested my head on the side of the building, forcing my heart to slow and my breathing to normalize. I had found her. I'd finally found Hope, and she was sitting mere feet away from me with nothing but a wall to separate us.

I glanced back into the window, careful to keep my face as hidden as possible. I knew for sure that the girl sitting there was Hope. I scanned the room but didn't see anyone else. My eyes darted toward the porch, but no one could see me from here. I was clear. If I took my chance now, I could get Hope out of there and away from the situation quickly, and Teddy would be able to handle the rest.

I didn't give it another thought. I knew it was something I had to do. It was now or never. I held my breath and scanned the area cautiously while I circled around to the side door. As I passed another window, I quickly checked again that Hope was alone. The best I could tell, she was. A mixture of emotions overcame me, sending my heart pounding and my hands shaking.

I nervously gripped the door handle but couldn't wait another moment. I rushed into the room and immediately over to Hope. She saw me instantly, and her eyes lit up.

"Hope!" I called, hurriedly crossing the garage to her corner. Her arms reached out toward me, and I swooped her up, cradling her in my embrace. I was ready to explain to her who I was and that I was there to save her, but I didn't have a chance before she spoke.

"Crystal!" she exclaimed excitedly.

My whole body tensed for a brief moment, but there wasn't time to ask her how she knew my name. All I knew was that I had to get out of there and back to the car before anyone realized I was missing from it. It hadn't even occurred to me to worry about where Lauren was right now. For all I knew, she had dropped Hope off here and left. The desire to get Hope to safety consumed me.

Hope and I pulled away from our embrace and gripped each other's hands. I didn't even get a chance to turn around before witnessing the terror fixed in Hope's eyes. Before she could shout a warning, something hard cracked into my skull. I crashed to the ground, and my vision went black in response to the ache pulsing through my head. The world swayed around me, and I couldn't make sense of which way was up and which way was down.

Objects across the floor blurred. Even after a few seconds when my vision returned, I couldn't understand what was going on. I quickly realized I was no longer holding Hope's hand. I knew I had to get up, but I still couldn't find my balance. I braced my palms against the concrete and strained to push myself from the cold surface. The room spun around me, and a high-pitched ringing assaulted my ears.

I finally found my way to a sitting position and cradled the area of impact with my left hand. My head reeled in a terrifying struggle to figure out what had just happened to me. I blinked a few times, and when my vision began to normalize, I looked around the room. A wooden board sat a few feet from me, and I instantly knew it was what hit me.

Then my eyes adjusted to find two figures standing in front of me. A woman with wild red hair held Hope against her body with one hand clamped down around her mouth.

Lauren, I thought, my mind full of spite for the woman. Every ounce of empathy I'd ever felt for her drifted away and was replaced with rage. I wouldn't stand by and let her beat me to a pulp, and there was no way I was going to let her hold onto Hope the way she was, not with the terror fixed in Hope's chocolate eyes.

"Stop it, Lauren," I demanded with every ounce of courage I could muster. I finally found enough sense of equilibrium that I stood from the floor. The task was harder than it sounded with the pounding headache and impaired sense of balance the blow had given me.

Lauren took a step back. Her eyes went wide, and it made me realize how crazy she actually looked. There was no doubt about it; Lauren needed some serious help. Unfortunately, I didn't have it in me to worry about helping her when Hope was shaking in terror. All I could think was that I hoped her mental state was stable enough that she wouldn't hurt Hope.

"How do you know my name?" Lauren demanded. "Who are you?"

"Just let her go," I insisted, taking a gentle step forward. Lauren only distanced herself from me, dragging Hope with her. "It's not worth it, Lauren."

"She's my little girl! I'd do anything for her." Lauren pulled in quick, shallow breaths with each step she took away from me. Just a few more feet and she'd be trapped against the back wall. She glanced around frantically until her eyes fell upon an object on the shelf behind her. She quickly grabbed for it and held the screwdriver out at me as if it were a sword. "Stay away from us," she threatened with a shaky voice.

"Just calm down," I tried as kindly as I could. "You know she's not your little girl. You know she's not Penny."

Lauren's face twisted into a cross between fear and anger. "How do you know about Penny?"

"I just do." I inched closer to her. "Now, let Hope go."

"Shut up. Just shut up!" Her eyes darted around the room, but she still held the screwdriver out at me. Her gaze fell upon me again as she spoke. "I don't know who you are, but you're not taking my little girl away from me again."

I kept her talking, hoping this might calm her down and she'd eventually release Hope. Frankly, I didn't have any other strength in this situation and didn't know what more to do. If I dove quickly, I might be able to grab ahold of the board she had used to hit me with, but I didn't think I had it in me to inflict physical pain on her, even as worry for Hope's sake washed over me.

"Why didn't you ever tell Scott about Penny?" I asked, partially to keep Lauren talking and partially out of my own curiosity. I knew she had tried to tell him the night before he left, but she never did. Maybe things would have turned out differently if she had told him and he'd been a part of their lives.

She narrowed her eyes at me like she couldn't quite place how I knew about her and Scott. Still, something about her demeanor changed as she reflected back on this time in her life. I almost thought I saw tears in her eyes, and she even dropped the screwdriver slightly when she spoke.

"He *left* me. I was going to tell him, but at the last minute, I decided I didn't want to make him choose between me and his father. So I let him worry about his dad for a while. After his dad died and he was done grieving, I was going to tell him, only *she* was already a part of his life, and they were getting *married*. Do you know how that made me feel?"

She didn't wait for an answer. "It's like he reached into my chest and ripped my heart out. The one man I ever loved was gone thanks to another woman. But how could I tell him then? I couldn't break apart a family like that, so I kept my distance."

"You didn't even tell him Penny died," I said to keep her talking.

"He didn't know about Penny at all. How could I tell him his daughter died when he didn't even know she existed?" Lauren's expression grew more sour as she talked. "What do you care anyway? And who are you?"

Her eyes narrowed at me the same time I opened my mouth to give her some lame excuse, but she spoke again before I could. "And why were you at my house?"

"Why did you destroy my car?" I retorted.

"It's because of you and your boyfriend that I had to bring her here. Your Minnesota license plate gave you away. We were fine before you came around looking for her."

Even as I spoke, I knew I should have been more afraid of Lauren. For some reason, I thought her wild eyes and disheveled look made her appear weak and scared even though she still held the screwdriver in front of her like it were a weapon.

"You can't keep running away, Lauren. There's a policeman here, and he's going to help get Hope home safely and get you the help you need."

"The police?" The hand holding the screwdriver came up to brush the hair out of her face, but the crazy look in her eyes remained. Suddenly, her eyes locked on me, and her entire stance shifted so that she was no longer rocking nervously. The screwdriver came out in front of her body again defensively when she realized what I was saying. "No, the police can't take her," she practically shouted. Her face twisted into an evil snarl.

"I'll be damned if someone is going to take my little girl again!"

In one quick motion, she spun Hope to the side to clear a path to me and twisted the screwdriver in her hand so she was holding it like a knife. And then she lunged.

25

A shriek escaped my lungs and reverberated off the walls of the garage as the screwdriver ripped through the skin on my left shoulder and Lauren's weight sent me crashing to the ground. I heard the crack of my phone as it crushed in my back pocket. Everything happened so fast that it was difficult to process.

Lauren gripped so tight onto the screwdriver that her knuckles turned white. She raised her arm above her head and thrust it down on me again. I tried to roll out of the way, but her body bore too much weight on my own. I squeezed my eyes shut, bracing myself for the second blow.

A second later, the blow still hadn't come, and then suddenly, Lauren's weight was lifted off me. I heard shuffling and opened my eyes just in time to see Robin's fist connect with Lauren's face. A little part of me rooted for him. He lunged for her again and pried the screwdriver — which she was now trying to assault him with — from her fingers. For a moment, I forgot how to move.

"Go," Robin shouted at me the same time he pinned down Lauren's flailing body.

I didn't waste another second. I quickly got to my feet and rushed over to Hope, who was crouched in the corner with tears streaming down her face.

"Come on," I prompted in a low voice.

Hope rushed to me immediately. I gripped her small hand, and together, we ran out of the garage toward the front of the house.

Teddy was already sprinting our way, no doubt in response to my scream. He slowed as he met up with us, and his eyes shifted from Hope to me then to my bloody shoulder. "Are you okay?" he asked frantically. Both of his hands came to grip my biceps, and his eyes stared seriously into mine.

"The garage," I said breathlessly, pointing behind the house with my good arm. Teddy immediately understood what I was saying and didn't waste another second. He ran off toward the garage.

Hope and I took off in the other direction at the same time. When we rounded the side of the house, the woman standing next to my mother finally processed what had happened in the last few seconds. I watched her fist come back, and I made a noise to warn my mother, but my mom was already shifting her weight. She dodged the punch and, in one swift movement, gripped the woman's wrist and twisted it around before pushing the woman's body up against the side of the house. The woman couldn't fight my mom off no matter how much she squirmed.

I came to a halt in witnessing this and stared in disbelief at my mother. I hadn't realized she was capable of that.

She caught a glimpse of my expression. "I took a self-defense class once," she explained. She cocked her head toward the car, and I understood immediately what she was trying to say.

I held on tight to Hope's hand and ran across the road, opening the door for her and helping her crawl into the passenger seat. I rounded the car and slid into the driver's seat. The keys I'd stuck in the ignition were still there, and even though I still didn't have my license, I was ready to make a quick getaway if needed.

"Are you okay?" I asked Hope. My chest rose and fell in time with my racing heartbeat.

Hope closed the gap between us and flung her arms around my neck. "I knew you'd save me. I just knew it! Thank you so much."

"Wait. What?" I asked as I pulled away from her. "How did you know? And how do you know my name?"

"I see you sometimes," Hope admitted slowly. "In my dreams. You're always there when I have nightmares about that night—the night she took me—and you're telling me that everything is going to be okay and that you're coming to get me. I knew you wouldn't let me down."

I couldn't move for several long seconds as I processed what she was saying. Every night that I'd dreamt about her abduction, she was reliving it, too. Only somehow, I was there with her. That phenomenon amazed me, but I didn't have the time to dwell on it for long. We were still in the middle of a crisis.

"It's not like she hurt me," Hope was saying. "I mean, she never tried to, but I was so scared. I miss my mom." Hope sniffled, wiping tears away from her face. "I hate it when she calls me Penny. I tell her that's not my name. She never believes me. Is it all over yet?"

I gazed past Hope to see if I could tell what was going on toward the house. I couldn't see anything but my mom holding the woman's body in place.

"Not yet," I told Hope. I reached into my pants pocket and pulled out my phone, desperately hoping it was still functional. I breathed a sigh of relief when the backlight came on. A crack ran the width of the screen, but I was still able to make a 911 call.

I never took my eyes off the yellow house while I spoke to the woman on the other end of the line. I had calmed down enough that I could make coherent sentences, but based on the woman's questions, I knew I wasn't quite making sense. I gave her the address I was at and said the word abduction enough times that I think she understood me. She assured me help was on the way and had me stay on the line until they arrived. When she asked if we needed an ambulance, I almost said no, but then the pain in my shoulder prompted me to answer yes. Besides, I had no idea how beat up everyone else was. Before I knew it, I could already hear the sirens.

"Are they coming to take me home?" Hope asked quietly.

I nodded. "Yes."

"Can't you take me home?"

I met her eyes. "I'm sorry. I don't think I can." Her face fell in a way that stung at my heart. "But I'll be back in Peyton Springs, and maybe if your mom lets us, we can spend some time together."

Hope's face lit up at my suggestion, but that only made me feel bad because I wasn't sure what would happen next. Her mom may choose to move away from where so much tragedy had happened recently, or maybe she simply wouldn't let anyone near Hope again. That's probably what I would do if my child was abducted.

I took a moment to examine my shoulder. My shirt was ripped, and a deep scratch ran up the front side of my deltoid. The screwdriver hadn't penetrated as deep as it could have but instead skidded along my skin. I didn't think I needed stitches, but the injury still stung and was lightly dripping with blood. I grabbed some tissues from the middle console and pressed them into my raw skin, biting back a cry of pain in the process.

I wrapped my good arm around Hope, glad this would soon be over for real. We both watched the police cars approach the house and shook nervously when they emerged from their vehicles. None of them noticed us right away. They first ran to my mother and the woman she was holding. I couldn't hear what was going on, even with the window cracked open, but I saw my mother release the woman, and her hands came up in a surrender stance. Her mouth moved, and then some officers raced around to the back of the house on their way to the garage.

A knock rapped at my window, and I nearly jumped out of my skin. I turned to find an officer standing above me. I hadn't even noticed him making his way over here. I quickly opened my door for him.

"Are you two okay?" he asked.

"I think so," I answered.

His eyes shifted to my injured shoulder and widened. "Our EMTs should take a look at that."

I nodded in agreement. The officer led me to the back of the ambulance, and an EMT tended to my shoulder while other officials questioned Hope.

I watched several officers lead a handcuffed Lauren around the side of the house. "She needs help," I said to no one in particular. My eyes remained locked on her.

The EMT followed my gaze. "Is she hurt?" she asked.

"I don't think so. Not physically. Ouch." I winced in pain when the EMT touched my shoulder. I could see a dark purple bruise forming now that some of the blood was gone. "She's sick. Mentally. That's why she took Hope. She needs to get psychiatric treatment."

The EMT nodded, but I didn't really think she was listening. She said I didn't need stitches but wrapped me up in gauze and tape instead. She also inspected the lump that was now forming on my head and questioned me about dizziness or nausea to be sure I didn't have a concussion. The pain had already passed except for a lingering headache, so I answered her honestly and assured her my head would be fine. She gave me an ice pack anyway. The whole time the EMT questioned me, I never shifted my gaze from Lauren until after they drove away with her.

Soon after I was properly bandaged, an officer came to ask me about what I had witnessed. I told as much of the truth as I could, bending it only so slightly. I explained how this was Teddy's case and that we'd been on vacation. Due to new information he'd received while on vacation—which I feigned ignorance to—he was compelled to check it out on his way back home. I told the officer that while Teddy left Robin and me in the car, I noticed motion behind the house, and, stupid little girl that I am, I went to check it out and found Hope and Lauren there.

I sounded innocent enough that I was positive he bought it. The rest of the events were the truth, only I left out the part about Hope telling me she knew me. I figured that would sound too suspicious, and I wasn't about to tell the officer about my abilities when I already knew he wouldn't believe that kind of story. So I stuck to what was most believable.

When I was finally free to go, I started toward Robin, except something in my peripheral vision caught my eye. Two figures stood on one side of the house, only they didn't quite fit the picture. Everyone else here was living, and I was the only one who could see them. I casually strolled toward Scott and Penny and leaned myself up against the house to make it look like I was still trying to recover, which in truth, I was.

I angled my body away from the crowd so people wouldn't see me talking to myself. "Is it all over, then?" I asked them.

They both smiled back at me. "I think so," Scott replied. "We can't thank you enough for rescuing Hope."

I offered a shy smile in return. "I couldn't have done it without either of you. You both led me to her. That's why I kept seeing you, Scott, wasn't it? In the hotel, gas station, and restaurant? You were trying to tell me I was getting closer to her, weren't you?"

Scott nodded.

"And you, Penny. You showed me where to go even though it seemed silly at the time."

Her smile widened in pride. "I couldn't cross over until I knew my mom was going to get the help she needed. I learned about Hope shortly before finding you. I'm glad we could help them both."

I looked between both of them. They really did look like father and daughter. It was painful to know they'd never had a chance to get to know each other and that Hope wouldn't grow to know her sister.

"It's okay," Penny said like she could read my thoughts, which I wasn't entirely sure was completely off from reality. "We get a chance to be together now, and someday, Hope will be with us, too."

They both shifted their gaze and looked at something I couldn't see.

"The light?" I asked.

Scott nodded while Penny smiled. "It looks like it," she said. "Thanks for helping my sister and my mom. I'm pretty sure she'll get the help she needs now."

"Always a pleasure," I replied. "Only, if you decide to ask for my help again," I joked, "could you not be all mysterious?"

"Will do," Scott agreed. Then he lifted his daughter onto his shoulders, waved goodbye, and walked into a light I couldn't see. They faded into nothing.

I smiled after them, happy that I could help them cross over and better their—for lack of a better word—lives. Unsure what to do next, I glanced around the lawn and locked eyes with my mother. She hugged me as soon as I was close enough.

"I thought we told you to stay in the car," she scolded, but I could hear relief in her voice.

"I'm sorry," I said guiltily, still locked in her embrace. "I couldn't just sit around."

"I know, sweetie. I know you're hurt, but I'm glad you took the initiative."

I pulled away from her in surprise. "You mean, you're not mad that I went to face Lauren alone?"

She shook her head. "I know mothers should be concerned about their child's safety, but I'm not your typical mother. You're a strong girl, Crystal, and I know that no matter what paths your abilities lead you on, you'll come away from each situation stronger than ever."

I didn't quite understand what had changed my mother's mind. A few weeks ago, she was scolding me for breaking into Tammy Owen's house to help my friend Kelli. Now she was praising me for breaking into someone's garage? I guess I proved to her that sometimes I had to break the rules to save people.

My mother paused for a moment and then continued. "We weren't getting much out of Colette — that was the girl's name who Teddy was questioning. It looked like Teddy was wondering if you made another mistake because it didn't make sense why Lauren would bring Hope here."

I still didn't understand it myself. "Why *did* she bring her here?"

"You can thank me for the answer to that," she told me proudly. "I asked Colette that same thing. Turns out Colette's daughter, Abby, and Penny were in the hospital at the same time, both for a heart condition, so Colette and Lauren got to know each other. I guess she was just a friend who understood her pain and was willing to take her in when she had nowhere else to go. Colette told me she'd lost Abby, too."

I dropped my head. A part of me still felt for Lauren's loss even though she'd attacked me. I couldn't imagine everything she'd been through with her daughter and her daughter's father dying around the same time.

I thought back to the funeral that I'd seen in a dream. "So, Jeff didn't have anything to do with this?" I asked.

"It doesn't look like it," my mom answered.

I looked over my mother's shoulder and caught a glimpse of Robin. I excused myself and made my way over to him.

His left eye was a dark shade of purple. He noticed me staring right away. "She got in one good punch," he explained.

"I'm so glad you're okay!" I exclaimed.

Robin pulled me into a gentle embrace. "Forget about me. What about you? How's your shoulder?"

"I'm fine," I answered, but the truth was that I was still a little shaken up.

"Fine enough that I can punch you?" He playfully punched my good shoulder.

"What was that for?" I asked, my voice rising a few notes above normal.

"For thinking you could handle something like that. Why didn't you wake me up? You may not have that nasty gash in your shoulder if you did."

My mouth twisted up guiltily. "I'm sorry." There was a brief moment of silence. "Hey, how did you know to save me anyway?"

"I didn't. I woke up and saw you were gone, only I could see you weren't with Teddy or Andrea, either. They didn't even notice when I went around the side of the house to look for you. I caught a glimpse of motion in the garage window, and then I heard you scream. When I went to check it out, you were getting your ass kicked."

"Hey," I defended playfully. "I ended up being fine."

"Only because I was there!" His arms came to wrap tighter around me again, pulling me to his chest. "I can't imagine what would have happened if I wasn't. She could have killed you, you know."

I hadn't thought about that, but I still wasn't entirely sure what lengths Lauren would go through to continue convincing herself that Hope was her daughter. Perhaps Robin was right. I was more thankful for him now than I'd ever been before.

"Thank you," I said softly, and then his lips came down to meet mine.

26

Tears streamed down my face. "Stop it, Robin!" My words were separated between my giggles. Robin's hands were clamped around my midsection, and he'd just found out how incredibly ticklish I am. I wriggled beneath him on my living room floor after we arrived home from our trip, but my attempts to flee were rendered useless.

"Teddy and I are leaving soon," I told him between giggles. "I have to get ready to go."

I screamed a high pitched yelp when his fingers found my most ticklish spot and dug in. I watched upside down as my mother entered the room and looked at us with an amused smile fixed on her face.

"Mom," I cried between laughs. "Tell him to stop."

"Robin," my mom scolded with a laugh.

Suddenly, his hands stopped moving, and I was finally able to catch my breath again.

"Sorry, Andrea," Robin said.

"Sorry? I was just going to say that you're doing it wrong." And then my mom bent to my level and tickled me under the arm pits. I screamed in laughter. Part of me wanted to kick each one of them in the face while another part of me was enjoying the fun.

The doorbell rang just then, and the hands tickling me pulled away. My mother leapt up from her crouch and headed toward the door while Robin and I dragged ourselves to the couch.

We still hadn't stopped laughing when I heard a familiar voice behind the door. "Emma!" I exclaimed, springing up to greet her.

My mother held the door open as Emma came into the house and crushed her body into mine in an embrace. I winced when she pressed against my bad shoulder, but I tried not to let the pain show through because I was too excited to see her. Besides, it wasn't as bad as it had been a few days ago. Derek followed behind Emma and gave me a light hug.

Emma bounced on the balls of her feet. "We missed you."

"I missed you guys, too."

"So, did you have fun on your vacation?" Derek asked.

"It was pretty good," I answered, unable to hide the bit of blush that was brewing in my cheeks as I thought about how close Robin and I had become in the last few days. I glanced at him quickly and realized how awkward this must be for all of them. "Uh, guys, this is Robin," I introduced.

"We met before," Derek pointed out, which made me feel a bit like a fool.

"Right," I said.

I watched my mom exit to the kitchen, and then I looked back to Emma. She was giving me a wide eyed look like she was trying to tell me something, only I didn't know what. I furrowed my brow in confusion.

"We need to talk," she whispered even though everyone else in the room could hear her. She gripped my arm and pulled me toward my bedroom. "You two get to know each other or something," she called back. "We'll be right back."

I could hear Derek behind us. "Must be a girl thing."

"What is it, Emma?" I asked once she shut the door to my bedroom.

"I have something to tell you, but you have to promise you won't get mad at me."

I narrowed my eyes suspiciously. What could she say that I would be mad about? "Um, okay. I won't get mad."

"Promise?"

I wasn't entirely sure because my psychic radar wasn't picking up on what she was about to say, so I didn't know if it was something I should be mad about or not. "I promise," I said anyway.

Emma pressed her lips together as if stifling a smile, and her cheeks flushed. I could even see the blush beneath her tan complexion. "Derek kissed me."

I smiled at her, partially out of happiness and partially because it was my duty as a best friend to tease her. I raised my eyebrows a little. "Ooh," I said, elongating the sound.

"You're not mad?"

"No, why would I be mad?"

Emma shrugged. "I don't know. I mean, I knew he kind of liked you for a while, and I still wasn't sure if you felt the same way about him."

"Derek? No."

"It's just," she continued, "we kind of had time to get to know each other on a personal level with you gone, and I don't mean that in a bad way—that you being gone was a good thing, but it kind of was." Emma bit her lip and didn't meet my gaze. "Finding his dog, spending Thanksgiving with him, it was all just so—"

"Emma," I stopped her. "It's fine. I'm with Robin now anyway, remember?"

She nodded. "I don't want you to feel like a third wheel or something."

"Emma," I put a hand on her shoulder and stared seriously into her eyes. "I'm fine with it."

A giant smile formed on Emma's face. "Thank you so much, Crystal." Emma surprised me with a hug so tight I could barely breathe.

"Calm yourself," I teased.

Emma rushed out of my room and back down the hallway. I followed. She raised both her thumbs in excitement. "She said yes!"

Derek's smile grew, and he hugged Emma. "That's great!"

It was a little weird to see them together like that, but if Emma was going to be with any guy, I was glad it was Derek.

Just then, Teddy entered the room. "Ready, Kiddo?" he asked.

"Ready," I said, grabbing my purse off the side of the couch. "Sorry, guys, but I have somewhere I have to be," I told Emma and Derek. "We can hang out later, okay?"

A few minutes later, Teddy and I arrived at the police station. Hope's mom, Melinda, said she wanted to thank me personally for helping rescue Hope, and Teddy agreed to mediate a session — not that we needed a mediator, but I felt more confident facing Hope's mom with Teddy there, especially since a part of me still felt guilty for not finding her sooner.

Happiness washed over me when I spotted Hope standing by her mother's side. It gave me extra reassurance that I really had rescued her and it wasn't all in my head. Hope looked mostly like her dad, but I could see now that she had Melinda's eyes.

Teddy introduced us. Immediately, Melinda's arms enveloped me. I grimaced as she squeezed my injured shoulder tight, but I knew she probably didn't know I'd been hurt, and if she did, she was probably too overcome with emotion to remember.

"Thank you so much." Her voice cracked, and I didn't need to look at her to see that tears were falling down her face. She pulled away and looked me in the eyes. "Hope tells me you were the one who found her. That's what the news has been saying, too, although they never mentioned you by name because you're a minor."

I nodded and gave her a reassuring smile. "Yeah, I did."

"I can't imagine. And what are the chances that you're from Peyton Springs, too?"

I shrugged because I didn't know what else to say. Surely I couldn't tell her it was all because of my abilities.

"Lucky, I guess. But I mean, Teddy was there, too, and he's been working on the case, so it's not that much of a coincidence." I was babbling, but I didn't want to have to explain myself, so I babbled instead.

Melinda wiped at her eyes. I looked down at Hope to see her smiling up at me and her hand held firmly against her mother's. It wouldn't surprise me if Melinda didn't let Hope go for a long time, which is why I was shocked with the next words that came out of her mouth.

"Hope won't stop talking about you. I'm looking for a babysitter who I can trust. My previous one is scared after what happened. I know I shouldn't let Hope out of my sight, but with Scott gone, I can't give up any extra work. Hope seems to really like you, so I thought maybe you'd be interested."

My jaw dropped in disbelief. I'd never imagined she would ask me this, and the thing was that I really liked Hope, too, and I knew we would have a blast together.

Melinda took my silence as a negative response. "It will only be a few hours every day after school. You would just have to pick her up from school and stay with her for two hours or so until I got home. You can have the weekends free."

"Please, Crystal," Hope begged. Her chocolate eyes widened until she looked like a sad puppy dog.

My shock only lasted another split second until I finally composed myself. "Yes!" I practically shouted. "I'd love to!"

Hope beamed at me, and I smiled back. After all the stress I went through to bring Hope home, I was glad I'd made a friend out of all of it. I could only wonder what I would gain from my next physic adventure.

ACKNOWLEDGEMENTS

To say that I published *Desire in Frost* by myself would be a lie. I had a lot of help along the way, and I can't thank these people enough.

To my team of beta readers, thank you for putting up with my constant questions and being honest with me. You all deserve a shout out: Heather, Deb, Cindy, Candy, Jan, Christin, Jason, Kelley, Jennifer, Anna, and Paul.

To my editor, Emerald Barnes, thank you for your constant encouragement and feedback along with your uplifting and inspiring attitude. And, of course, thank you for catching my silly mistakes!

A huge thank you to Clarissa Yeo for her fantastic artwork on the covers.

Finally, I can't thank fans and readers enough for encouraging me to continue the series and for leaving their reviews on Amazon and Goodreads.

ABOUT THE AUTHOR

Alicia Rades is a freelance writer, blogger, and editor. When inspiration strikes, she is also an author. Alicia has been captivated by the YA paranormal and supernatural genre since reading *The Seer* series by Linda Joy Singleton when she was 12 years old. The Crystal Frost series was born out of the love for the genre and is Alicia's first series. In college, Alicia majored in professional writing. Alicia lives in Wisconsin with her husband and too many fish to count.